THE ALPHA STRAIN

An Alex Hunt Adventure Thriller

URCELIA TEIXEIRA

Independently Published
Urcelia Teixeira

To my mother who taught me perseverance and respect for all people. Whose inner strength through adversity has been a lamp unto my feet.

To my husband — my #1 supporter, muse, best friend and partner in life. Your unwavering belief in my writing thrusts me onward and upward.

Receive a FREE copy of the prequel and see where it all started!

NOT AVAILABLE ANYWHERE ELSE!

Click on image or enter http://download.urcelia.com in your browser

CHAPTER ONE

FEBRUARY 11TH, 1990 - VICTOR VERSTER PRISON, SOUTH AFRICA

Johan Theron gripped his young son's hand as the crowd on the opposite side of the road threatened to push through the barricades and police officials. They were among the thousands of people that had gathered along the hip-high metal fences surrounding the prison - whites on the left, blacks on the right. Johan smiled lovingly at his wife and kissed the back of her hand. They've never been out together in public, and for the first time since they were married, he saw a future for the three of them. It was the happiest day of his life; one that held no boundaries.

"Thandi, my love, this is it. We don't have to hide anymore. This is the day we've been praying for. Tomorrow I'm taking you to that fancy restaurant on Adderley Street, and I'm going to buy you the nicest dress from the boutique down the road; and that's only the beginning. We'll go to the drive-in theatre in *one* car and watch that new Bond movie you've been talking about. Just

1

like we dreamed about. And our little boy over here, will go to the best private schools, and he'll be allowed at any of the country's top universities; just like everyone else in this country."

Thandi smiled back at her husband of eight years. Hope filled her eyes as she listened to her husband's dreams about their future. Their marriage hadn't been easy. Living amongst a nation where black and white people were separated from each other by law proved harder than they initially thought it would be. Their marriage was known only to her family who saw no distinction between them. They had been in hiding on the farm since the day they met and fell in love. Johan was the son of a white cattle farmer, and Thandi, the daughter of one of his father's black workers on their family farm. And their young son, neither white nor black. Apartheid laws prevented them from being seen together, much less being married. And, if caught, would have them killed. But not anymore. This day marked the end of Apartheid in South Africa. Where no law nor man will have the right to discriminate against any race. Where blacks and whites could buy from the same shops and sit on the same busses together, and where Johan Theron, a white farmer could freely hold his black wife's hand in public.

The crowd cheered louder as the massive prison gates opened and the police officials ushered Nelson Mandela to freedom.

Johan protectively scooped his four-year-old son up into his arms as the crowds forced their way to the front to get a better view of the man that will set the nation free.

He watched his fellow white nationals looking on in somber silence. They knew this day would change their lives forever. The white people of South Africa had relinquished their reign to a black government that harbored decades of hatred and oppression against them. The tides had turned and once rulers of a predominantly white country will now be no more. Johan searched his heart. Covered under a blanket of guilt over being party to it all, he was torn between his white heritage and own hopes for a new future with his black wife and colored child. Until now he had been stuck between two opposite worlds that will today become one.

His inner convictions were interrupted as a multitude of triumphant black citizens broke out into loud applause and proudly waved their homemade banners above their heads. Clicking their tongues in tribal chime, they saluted Mandela as he slowly made his way down the long driveway toward the cheering crowd of supporters. The Theron family and the rest of the world watched as Nelson Mandela walked out of prison a free man.

A young television news reporter and his cameraman moved closer to the crowd against the barrier in front of Johan. His voice was filled with uncertainty masked by words of pride and feigned excitement.

"And there he is South Africa, Mr. Nelson Mandela. Freed after twenty-seven years in prison and now a beacon of hope to a new nation. It is a historic day for our country as this man holds the hope of the nation on his shoulders; a new nation. No longer separated by the color of our skin, but united as one nation. As he walks toward us, excited supporters of the African National Congress welcome their new leader taking his first steps into a new South Africa. And the unspoken question on everyone's lips remains. What will this mean to the white South African?"

"VIVA MANDELA! AMANDLA!" An excited crowd shouted as Mandela got into his chauffeured vehicle and drove off along the crowded street. Masses of supporters pushed each other out of the way fighting for a chance to touch his car. Struggling to control the hordes, police officials moved their shields into their trained formation in an attempt to push a large number of overly enthusiastic supporters away from the car. On the far end, a large group of white protestors shouted in anger as they expressed their disagreement with Mandela's release.

Subdued sniffing had Johan turn around to see a proud Afrikaans man behind him. He was older, in his late fifties perhaps and dressed in traditional farmer attire — khaki shorts, button-up short-sleeve khaki jacket and a matching khaki hat. The white-bearded man wiped his eyes.

"What are you looking at, traitor?" the man spat at Johan, who turned back around and ignored him. Johan gripped Thandi's hand and held onto his son.

"Hey! I said. What are you staring at, you traitor? You, with your black slave-wife and bastard son! You're a disgrace to this country! What? Do you think you are better than us now that you can take your black slave into our streets?"

Johan clenched his jaw as he fought the urge to defend his wife and son's honor. His body grew tense under the man's insults.

He sensed things were about to get ugly. His eyes frantically searched for a way out through the masses of people flanking both sides of him.

"So now you're a coward too? Fight back like a man. Or have you forgotten you're white?"

The farmer's words precipitated his friends huddling closer together, preventing Johan and his family from moving in either direction to escape his wrath. They were trapped between an angry group of white farmers and the barricade. Johan felt his pulse quicken as he pulled his son closer to his chest and whispered in his ear. "If something happens you run to that policeman there and you ask him to take you to Gôgo on the farm, ok?" Knowing his son was tiny enough to slip through the metal bars he pointed to a colored official about twenty yards ahead on the other side of the bulwark.

The reporter who had his back toward them, turned around as he became aware of the commotion that was playing out in the crowd behind him. With the camera pointed at his face, a now frightened Johan stared directly into the lens. He knew full well the danger that threatened their mixed-race family. But with no way out, Johan pinned his faith on the camera lens in the hope that it might intimidate the angry white man behind him. He was wrong. Seconds later he felt the sharp edge of a knife in his right shoulder and stumbled forward against the iron roadblock. His son fell forward onto the reporter who caught him just in time before a second stabbing sliced into Johan's bicep. From the corner of his eye, he noticed police officials charging toward them.

"You'll never be white, you black whore!" someone yelled

behind him just before he heard Thandi's shrill scream as she dropped to her knees.

"Thandi!" Johan screamed and stooped down to help her up.

Warm liquid instantly drenched his hand under the stab wound in his wife's ribcage. Rubber bullets flew over his head onto the attackers behind them as the police stepped in to break up the assault. Concerned only for his wife he ignored his own injuries and pulled Thandi to her feet, lifting her over the metal barricade. He had to get his wife and son to safety. He let go of Thandi for a moment to take his son from the reporter's arms when a gunshot echoed through the air and hit his wife in her neck. Thandi Theron slumped onto the tarmac beside him. He watched in shock and horror as life drained from his beloved wife's brown eyes. She was barely breathing. Blood gushed from her neck.

"Help! Somebody, help!" he screamed while the police charged into the crowd to detain the shooter.

He knelt down and stared at the open bullet wound in Thandi's neck. The pressure from his large hand on the wound provided little resistance as blood pumped through his shaking fingers out onto the ground. The terrifying sobs of his young son crying in fear beside him sent chills through his body.

"Hold on Thandi, hold on! I'm going to get you to a doctor. Don't you dare die on me today! Do you hear me? Not today! Today is our day of freedom. Don't you die on me, Thandi!"

Johan scooped his wife up in his arms and, with his son clinging to his leg, ran toward the prison gates. Chaos ensued as the events set off a motion of protests between black and white citizens. But Johan's tense gaze looked straight ahead at the prison gates in front of him. Determined it was the only place he might find medical assistance he pushed through his physical pain and rushed toward the entrance. Wedged between the police and the protestors, Johan ducked as rubber bullets flew over his head.

"Sir, this way!" The reporter shouted, pulling both Johan and his son into the safety of their news van. With the help of the reporter and his cameraman, they lay Thandi on the floor inside the van. A soft groan escaped her blood-filled mouth.

"Shh, try not to speak. We're going to get you to a hospital. Just hold on, ok?"

But Johan's pleas and his young son's cries weren't enough to prevent the inevitable and Thandi Theron drew her last breath.

As Johan Theron poured the last spade-full of sand over Thandi's casket, a fresh tear rolled down his cheek. He sat down on the loose soil next to his son and pulled him into his arms. The sun hung low on the horizon of his farm in the North-West province of South Africa, and for the first time, he had no hope. Encircled by the whimpers of her friends and family, and the soft singing of a tribal hymn, as the sun's last rays hit his face, Johan Theron's soul died.

"It will be ok, Pa. I'll look after you" his young son's words of childlike strength chimed in his ears. "You can sleep with me in my bed ,and I'll let you hold Mr. Teddy."

Johan looked into his son's eyes and saw the innocence of an evil world yet unknown to him. He had no idea of the political significance of his mother's death. Perhaps it was best that way. Best that he never knew she got killed because she wasn't white. And while his heart ached for the life they dreamed of, he had to protect his son from the same ridiculed fate. Resolved to shave his son's curly ash brown hair, and rub lemon juice on his skin to make it paler, Johan silently vowed to never let the world find out the truth. He would raise him as a white man and no one would ever know he was the son of a white man and a black woman.

CHAPTER TWO

PRESENT DAY

Alex closed the door behind her and paused on the pavement outside her apartment. Shutting her eyes for a minute, she breathed in the crisp spring air. She was more than content with life. Having finally moved out of her parents' home and into her own apartment, Alex felt liberated. And for the first time in her life, she was free to explore the woman of strength she had become. But when Sam declared his love for her, extending their relationship beyond the borders of their friendship, she knew they could no longer work together. Motivated by her strong convictions to keep business separate from their personal lives she left the university's Archaeology faculty and took on a more senior position with a private antiquities recovery firm in London. It was a bold step outside the safe boundaries the university provided her, but she was ready. Leaving the university sealed her newfound confidence in life and propelled her career into an exhilarating new direction in the private sector. She no longer spent days lecturing or accompanying students on digs unearthing ancient artifacts for European museums. Instead, her days were spent recovering and returning looted or lost artifacts; determining their authenticity and origin. But with it came a new set of perils on her expeditions as she worked closely with local governments and cultural heritage associations across the globe. It was challenging at times but highly rewarding, and she loved it.

Sam had more than proved himself capable and, upon Alex and her father's personal recommendation, stepped into her Head of Archaeology position at the university. They were happy together, and their relationship reached a depth akin to that of being soul mates.

A lex smiled broadly as she began the short walk to the bus stop.

"Miss Hunt." A stern male voice spoke behind her. Alex turned to lay eyes on a tall, athletic-built man dressed in a black suit and tie. His eyes were shielded by black sunglasses, and in his left ear, she spotted an earpiece with its cord running down the back of his neck disappearing beneath his collar. He stood beside an open door of a black luxury SUV.

"Miss Hunt, please step inside the vehicle," the man spoke again, and this time Alex picked up his strong American accent.

"Why? Who are you?" she questioned with trepidation.

"Ma'am, it's a case of international importance. Please come with me?"

"International importance? What do you mean? Who are you?"

"It will all be explained to you, Miss. Please step inside the vehicle."

Alex searched the vehicle's interior, keeping her distance from the open door. Apart from the chauffeur and this man, the car was empty. She discreetly squeezed her elbow against her hip where she carried her firearm. Something Sam insisted she had on her at all times considering the nature of her new job. She wasn't sure if it was a mere case of curiosity, but when the strange man in black nudged her again to get in, she did.

The red leather seats and a fitted silver tray with a crystal carafe and two whiskey glasses reeked of luxury. The car's windows were tinted black and remained closed as the suited stranger took his place in the front passenger seat next to the chauffeur. She fiddled with her window's electronic button to let some air in, but it was locked. This vehicle didn't belong to her employer. That much she knew. Perhaps it was sent by one of their new clients. She retrieved her mobile phone from her purse with the intention of calling her boss when the man in black suddenly turned to face her.

"Please refrain from using your mobile phone, Miss Hunt. We can't afford a leak."

A leak? A leak of what? Who the hell are these people? She thought. Her heart skipped a beat as she put the phone back inside her handbag and peered through the window for the remainder of their ride. When the vehicle pulled up twenty minutes later to a modern gray building in the center of London, Alex was somewhat relieved to see she hadn't been taken to an obscure warehouse somewhere in the middle of nowhere. Closed circuit cameras surrounded the large black steel gate, and four guards on duty were each armed with semi-automatic rifles. As the car pulled up to the gate, the guards didn't stop their car or ask for any security clearance. Instead, one of them promptly opened the gate and let them through.

"This way, Miss Hunt," the man in black ushered Alex through the large glass doors at the front of the building, passing several more armed guards before being stopped at the walk-through metal detector.

"Are you carrying any firearms or weapons?" Another guard asked.

Alex caught her breath as the thought of surrendering her only safety measure sent a shiver down her spine. She considered taking a chance, praying that by some miracle the machine wouldn't detect her firearm.

"Ma'am, please place your firearm in the basket and proceed through the scanner."

Her face must have betrayed her intentions to conceal her gun. Irritated, Alex conceded by unclipping her Smith and Wesson 9 mm pistol from her holster. With a now practiced hand, she released the magazine and emptied the chamber into the container on the table. Once through the scanner, a female guard stepped up to her and body-searched her further. With her pistol tagged and locked in a safe behind the table, the man in black beckoned for her to get into a glass elevator. Alex tightened her shaking hands around the handle of her purse in front of her as she watched the digits on the elevator panel climb thirty-five floors. She dared not challenge her fear of heights by looking out the clear window behind her. Her stomach was already in a knot. The secrecy around the motive for her presence gripped her insides. She still had no idea where she was, or what she was doing there. All she knew was that whoever these people were, their security was extensive and they seemed to be American.

W hen the elevator doors opened, Alex, stepped out into an expansive office surrounded on three sides by clear floor to ceiling glass windows overlooking London. The man in black stayed behind in the elevator, and Alex soon heard the doors close behind her. At the far end, a group of men was seated at a large glass boardroom table. Unsure of the meeting she had been thrust into, she slowly walked to where the small party hung onto every word spoken by a man dressed in an expensive steel-gray three-piece suit; their attention held captive as if under hypnosis. The distinguished man's ability to command the room was evidence of his authoritative power and influence beyond what she's ever seen.

"Ah, Miss Hunt, glad you could join us," the man's deep voice and heavy American accent cut through her thoughts.

"Allow me to introduce myself. Matthew Fletcher, most people just call me Matt. Please, come in and take a seat."

Matt pulled out a black leather boardroom chair next to him at the head of the table. As if recited, the remaining men around the table immediately introduced themselves one by one — A scientist, paleoanthropologist, Air Force general, and a Frenchman whose title she couldn't quite make out.

"Can I offer you something to drink, Miss Hunt?" Matt didn't wait for her to answer and signaled his assistant to pour her a cup of tea from a fresh pot that stood on a nearby table. Alex didn't take the seat he pulled out for her. It was evident everyone jumped at his every command, and she needed to make a stand at the onset.

"Mr. Fletcher, I —"

"Matt, please. Everyone just calls me Matt," he cut her short.

"Ok, Matt, I'm not one to pass my valuable time with insignificant pleasantries, so can you please tell me why I was brought here and who you are exactly?"

Matt's lips curled into a slight smile over her directness. Then folding his hands on top of the table, he leaned in and adopted a more serious look in his eyes.

"Alex," he started "May I call you Alex?"

Again he continued without an answer from her.

"We brought you here because we need your help. Now before we continue, I need you to turn off your mobile phone, please?"

At this point, Alex didn't find anything surrounding the situation strange anymore and, taking her seat, somehow did precisely what he told her to do.

"Welcome to ICCRU, Alex."

His declaration caught Alex somewhat off guard.

"ICCRU? What business do I have with the International Cultural Crimes Recovery Unit?" she prompted, surprised at how calm her voice was.

"I'm impressed. You've heard of us then?"

"I wouldn't be doing my job properly if I didn't, Mr. Fletcher."

"Well, then you would also know that we take our work very seriously and while we are in a similar line of business as you, our powers extend far beyond any private sector recovery firm. We have the authority of the CIA, FBI, MI6, and Interpol behind us, not to mention the UN, Military, Navy, and Air force units of any country we so choose. Let's just say we're quite a bit more senior than the small firm you find yourself at".

The corners of his lips curled up as he paused. Alex didn't answer. Instead, she took a sip of her tea, praying her internal trembling wouldn't betray her composed facade.

Matt cleared his throat and continued. "And while our firm has a highly skilled hand-picked and trained task force, and we go to great lengths to avoid involving outside parties in our assignments, we have become aware of your unparalleled reputation. It appears that your unique abilities make you the only candidate equipped and experienced enough to handle this particular crisis we find ourselves in. Now, my team will brief you on your mission, and you will have ICCRU's full support no matter what, but you should clear your schedule. We deploy in three days."

Alex placed her empty teacup back on the table and cleared her throat.

"Mr. Fletcher, while I appreciate the weight your establishment carries, and deem myself flattered with your gracious offer, I think you ought to tell me exactly what mission you're presuming I'd push my paying clients aside for and jump to accept instead. With all due respect, I'm not easily intimidated or impressed by credentials, and frankly, the secrecy under which I was coerced to come here, leaves much to be desired."

A few of the men around the table fought back the urge to laugh at her audacious statement, fully aware of the fact that no-one ever took the liberty of declining anything Matthew Fletcher set before them.

Equally amused, Matt's mouth curled into the slightest of smiles as he moved around his chair and positioned himself in front of the large windows to admire the bird's eye view of the city below. But his amusement soon turned to a stern voice by which he conveyed he wasn't about to take no for an answer.

"Mark, I think you'd better explain the situation to Miss Hunt before she assumes she has a choice in the matter."

"Of course, Matt," the paleoanthropologist immediately responded.

Dr. Mark Davies clicked a small black remote and excitedly took up position next to the projector screen on the wall behind Alex.

"Miss Hunt, meet *Homo naledi*. The world's first and only hominin, or in layman's terms, the closest relation to our current human species."

Alex watched as the projector flashed an image of an odd

looking combination of a modern man merged with a more primitive one across the screen. Though an artist's rendering, it appeared bizarrely lifelike.

"This remarkable discovery was made in 2013 during a recreational cave exploration just outside Johannesburg, South Africa. It bears a significant historical discovery that completely turns the evolutionary biology on its head. Over 1500 skeletal bones were excavated and now provide conclusive evidence of a unique human species that was, up until now, completely unknown to us. And I'm sure you can see the remarkable resemblance to humans as we are today. In fact, it took two more years to fully excavate, but our tests prove this is by far the closest relation to the human genus found to date. Further analysis shows us that it's also the youngest species at somewhere between two hundred thousand and three hundred thousand years old. It's as close to our human ancestral family tree as we can get! And although the thorax is primitive and appears more ape-like than human, its hands, in contrast, are shaped more modern which meant they were well equipped to making basic tools. Now, his feet indicate he walked upright, while his fingers appear to be more curved, a feature only seen in apes that spend most of their time in trees."

"All right Mark, simmer down." Matt interrupted before finally taking his seat behind the table and continuing the brief.

"Our doctor here can get a tad carried away with obvious excitement over this, so let me get to the crux of the matter. It's the most unique human ancestral species found to date. Nothing like it exists anywhere else on the planet and it's crucial we preserve it at all costs. As Mark alluded to, it pushes the boundaries on evolution as we know it and proves early man to be more similar to what we look and behave like today versus the original hypotheses that we were all ape-man and Neanderthals. And that's where you come in Alex. You need to find the last piece of the missing link."

CHAPTER THREE

Alex listened intently as Matt Fletcher and his team explained the mission. Archaeology was and always would be in her blood, and the longer the brief continued, the harder it was for Alex to deny that his proposal excited her beyond measure. Opportunities to have a hand at finding a missing puzzle piece to the human origin family tree were rare. However, as good as she was at her job, and as much as this project enthused her, she sensed there was much more to the quest than what she was being told.

Desperate for solitude to digest the information, Alex escaped Matt's powerful gaze and took her turn looking at the city view from the window. Conscious of the team's piercing stares on her back in anticipation of her acceptance, she broke the silence and turned to address the men at the table behind her.

"Gentlemen, it's tempting, I confess, but I don't quite understand. If the remains of Homo *naledi* were already discovered and excavated, it seems you merely need to send one of your teams to Johannesburg and retrieve it yourself. I don't understand why you need *me*. If it's a mere case of getting down into the cave to excavate the fossil in question, why not just get a team to go down and get it?"

No one spoke as her question hung thick in the air.

"We already tried, Alex. We can't find it. What's more is that we now have reason to believe the head of the excavation team already retrieved and hid it somewhere."

"So why not just ask the man where it is?" Alex continued.

"He's dead, Alex. Professor Graham was found bludgeoned to death in his office. We suspect whoever did this was after the fossil and Professor Graham must have intentionally concealed its location to protect it from landing up in the wrong hands. Problem is, he never told anyone else where he hid it."

A moment later the short stocky man with the outlandish accent spoke for the first time.

"Miss Hunt, given the sensitive nature of this assignment it would be our duty to support you throughout the entire mission. Your safety is of primary concern to us".

"Safety! You haven't the foggiest idea who killed the professor and if they found whatever they killed him for or not? How the hell do you intend keeping me safe Mr....?"

"Jean-Pierre DuPont, official representative for UNESCO," the French man introduced himself.

Stunned with his introduction, Alex went silent.

"That's United Nations Educational, Scientific and Cultural

Organization; headquartered in Paris." DuPont added assuming her silence meant she didn't know what UNESCO was. "We are largely responsible for building global peace and security. We're also the ones who appointed ICCRU to intervene and handle this particular mission for us."

"I know what UNESCO is Mr. DuPont." Alex paced the room as she listened to the French delegate ramble on about his agency. Mr. DuPont's accent was too heavy for Alex to fully understand his every word, but when the United Nations was involved in anything it usually meant serious business. Alex rubbed her fingers over her brows.

"Mr. DuPont, why would this mission require the UN to intervene? A man was killed over a human fossil that's now presumed stolen. Seems it's a simple case of solving a murder, that's all."

The group of men shuffled uncomfortably around the table. It was the scientist in his crisp white lab coat's turn to speak for the first time.

"It's not just any fossil, Miss Hunt. We're talking about an extremely unique hominin species we believe can prove ancestral heritage dating back to Adam and Eve. Our recent genetic research suggests that all females are descended from a single female and all males from a single male, which is consistent with the Biblical portrayal of Adam and Eve. We believe the missing fossil piece contains, what we refer to as the mitochondrial gene that will link humanity all the way back to the Garden of Eden! I think it goes without saying what an immense impact it will have on the entire world if our human lineage traces us back to Eve itself. But if it gets destroyed or buried forever, we might never have another opportunity to prove the primary biblical concept the entire world thinks is just a myth. We're pinning science against religion, Miss Hunt!"

Matt cleared his throat signaling a man with a well decorated uniform seated at the other end of the table to speak.

"General Willie Dreyer, South African Air Force Ma'am," the man in a blue uniform with a strong South African accent introduced himself. "Unfortunately there are additional strenuous circumstances complicating the situation even further, Miss Hunt. The political climate in South Africa has taken a turn for the worse. The opposing political parties have created much division across the nation and civilians have taken things into their own hands. The South African people have overthrown the presidency and we now find ourselves in the throngs of a civil war. The country has quite literally gone haywire and the excessive violence and public uproar is making it nearly impossible to get any archaeology teams on the ground. We will provide safe entry and exit into our country with the help of the South African Defense Force and the UN, but the rest is up to you. We already have a dedicated special task force to accompany you at all times on standby awaiting our 'go'."

The Air Force general's words left Alex cold.

"Civil war? Have you all lost your minds? I'm in no way equipped to fight in a war. Caving for fossils, sure, but being thrust in the middle of a war with a faceless murderer after the same thing? That's preposterous!"

Matt met up with Alex where she was still pacing the length of the window.

"We're not looking for bones, Alex. We've successfully managed to rescue all one-thousand-five-hundred-and-fifty bones that had been excavated from the cave back in 2013. We're looking for the molars; or at least one and at this stage we're not sure if it's still in the cave. Fact is, Alex, we have lost all contact with our previously deployed team and new Intel suggests they might have never made it to the check-in point in the first place. If there was anyone else we thought equipped enough to handle this mission, we would have sent them. There isn't. You're the best at tracking down relics, and your proven combat skills make you the ideal candidate to retrieve possibly the biggest piece of history yet. The professor had some eccentric methods. He was known to be very fond of encrypting anything he thought was of value and this is one of those things. It's so deeply hidden not even his closest colleagues are able to find it and all the leads we had up to this point ran dead. We're missing something and I'm told you have a knack for cracking these things. You're our only hope at finding the molar and bringing it home."

"So let me get this straight. You're asking me to somehow figure out where the professor hid the teeth in the midst of a full blown civil war, run the risk of getting killed all the while not knowing who I'm up against?"

Matt nodded. "The world needs you, Alex."

Alex paused as Matt Fletcher's eyes conveyed the seriousness of the situation. But, beyond the distinguished layer of power and business, his eyes revealed a tenderness she didn't think existed. One that contradicted his all-about-business exterior, and instead, revealed a heart filled with passion for a cause she too shared. The risks were enormous, but proving biblical maternal lineage would rewrite history. Her archaeological expertise was superior, and her survival and combat capabilities sharpened by the best instructors the British army offered. If ever she were ready for an assignment of this magnitude, this would be it. Once again she turned away from him and stared at the city through the window. Her heart pounded hard against her chest as she heard herself reply.

"I'm going to need my colleague on this too; that's a non-negotiable."

Alex heard several sighs of relief coming from the men at the table as Matt replied.

"I expected as much. Arrangements have already been made to include Dr. Quinn." Matt smiled in victory and slapped his palms together as he motioned the dismissal of the meeting.

"Let's make it happen, gentlemen. We reconvene tomorrow morning to finalize the logistics."

Matt hurried across the room and summoned his assistant from the phone on his desk before looking up at Alex again.

"You're doing the right thing, Alex. This is your chance to show the world how far you've come. We'll make sure you're properly prepared. I'll have Duncan drop you off at your apartment so you can get your affairs in order. Your boss has already been informed, so no need to go into the office. Someone in my team will pop by your apartment over the next twenty-four hours to deliver your gear and brief you on the details of your departure. I'll leave it up to you to bring Dr. Quinn up to speed on the matter."

Alone at her apartment Alex pulled her duffle bag from her closet and started to pack. The events of her day was a blur — as if she was in a deep sleep she might not have woken up from yet. Thinking about it now she realized she never had a snowball's chance in hell of *not* agreeing to the assignment. That much was evident when she phoned her boss who confirmed Matt had already been in touch with him and that her work was taken care of. Matthew Fletcher was a man who got what, and who he wanted, no matter what.

It was almost dinnertime and Sam was due to arrive any moment. She silently prayed he'd be as enthused about the mission as she was. It was after all any archaeologist's dream. She tried not to let her mind ponder on the dangers involved and allowed the thrill of discovering the world's first evidence of mitochondrial Eve smother her fears.

An hour later, Sam arrived and spotted her bag on the floor at the front door. "Going somewhere, sweetheart?" planting a passionate kiss on her lips. "Hope you were planning on a decent goodbye before you upped and left?" he playfully nuzzled her neck.

"What makes you think I'm going anywhere without you?" She flirted back and walked to the kitchen to pour him a glass of wine.

"Oh, so you planned a little dirty weekend away for us some-where? Then why pack anything at all?"

"You have such a wicked mind, Sam Quinn. But as it happens, it might very well get a little dirty, and actually, it would be a tad longer than just a weekend".

Alex carried the bowl of pasta to the dining table as Sam followed sporting a sheepish smile across his face. She loved how close they have become in their relationship.

"Anything significant happening at the Uni at the moment? Think you can clear your schedule?" Alex asked.

"For a dirty weekend away with you, any day! Why? What's up?"

Sam tucked into his dinner as Alex tried to find the best way of getting him on board.

"How would you like to help me find out if Adam and Eve and the whole Garden of Eden hypothesis is fact or fiction?"

Sam put his fork down and took a large sip of wine. "That big, huh? You don't play around with your expeditions lately do you, Alex, my love? Is the Pope Catholic?" He mocked sarcastically. "Of course, you know I wholeheartedly believe in the truth of the Holy Bible, so digging up evidence to prove it — why not? What evidence are we looking for here, though?"

Relieved she had him hooked she quietly deliberated whether to let him in on the dangers of the mission or to just leave it be. Deciding she'd amplify the archaeological significance first, she ignored his question and spent their entire dinner telling him all about *Homo naledi* and what she'd managed to Google on the subject so far.

"I'm expecting the full brief to come through tomorrow, so we'll know more then, but what do you say? Can I count you in? I can't do this one without you, Sam."

Noticing the hint of fear in Alex's voice, Sam raised his glass. "Here's to making history, my beloved. To you, me and Africa; once again! Now, when do we leave? I will let Professor Keating know first thing tomorrow. He'll be thrilled to have the University involved."

"Not going to be possible, Sam. He can't know anything. No one can. Not even your mother. This assignment is top-secret. As in, you, me and these four walls 'top-secret'. Understand?"

"Gee woman! You sound serious. What's the big deal?"

Alex rose and walked across to the kitchen to get another bottle of wine. Her heart pounded heavily under the knowledge of needing to declare the full mission to Sam.

"The mission is a tad more complicated than anything we've attempted before, Sam. It's an ICCRU mission and...well, the United Nations is behind it. Our conditions will be somewhat of a challenge".

"Go on." Sam urged her as he pulled the cork from the wine bottle.

Alex cleared her throat and took a deep breath. "South Africa is at war, Sam. A massive politically charged one at that. As far as I know it's racially motivated and goes back to apartheid."

"So what you're saying is we'd be dropped in a war zone."

"Yup."

"How violent is it?"

"Don't know. Apparently it's really bad. The previous team never made it to the check-in point. The conditions aren't clear at the moment, but I have the assurance of the South African air and military forces that they will be taking every measure to ensure our safety. We're expected to leave in forty-eight hours. Our full briefing is tomorrow."

Sam downed his glass of wine. "And what exactly do we need to retrieve?"

"Teeth, the molars to be exact. It's been proven the molars are most effective in DNA testing."

"Teeth! You might as well tell me we need to find that proverbial needle in a haystack on Old MacDonald's farm. Where would we even start?"

"I don't think I'm equipped to handle this one without you, Sam. I need someone I trust to have my back, and well, you're him. I know it's going to be a bit of a challenge, but with the army protecting us, we just follow the clues. Nothing we haven't done before. "

Sam sat back in his chair and marveled at the excitement in Alex's eyes. "Let's do it! We have nothing to lose and everything to gain, my love. The way I see it, we have the opportunity of a lifetime!"

CHAPTER FOUR

Alex tightened the military aircraft's seat belt over her shoulders and double-checked the three-point buckle around her waist. This assignment had her more restless than any of their usual missions and she found it difficult to settle in on the flight. The thunderous power of the airplane's engines brought little solace as she eyed the short line of seated combat soldiers opposite her. Eight in total. Most of them were in their twenties; someone's son, husband or brother. She wondered if she'd ever have it in her to see her child go off to fight a war. Sitting shoulder to shoulder with them in a combat plane was upsetting enough let alone waiting months on end never knowing if they'd return home.

She wasn't sure why this mission had her so restless. Perhaps it was the fear of the unknown. She had never been in a war zone before. The ICCRU briefing said little about the current conditions once they landed in Johannesburg. Her mind recalled the images of Iran that had been on BBC news channel that morning. It wasn't something she'd want to experience. She forced it out of her mind and tried to focus on something else. Amid her angst she managed to curl the corners of her mouth into a slight smile as her eyes met the blank eyes of the soldier's gaze directly opposite her. He didn't react. Instead, his eyes looked right through her. Like he was in some kind of a trance. She shuffled uncomfortably as it left her somewhat embarrassed. These soldiers were trained to block their minds and not feel anything. Adjusting the noise protection earphones that were at a minimum two sizes too big for her head, she looked down the row to the next soldier. Determined to find at least one soldier who showed some emotion, she allowed her eyes to follow the line of combat troops down the wall of the fuselage, but they all had the same motionless stares on their faces; ostensibly in the same psyched realm as the one opposite her. She forced herself not to ponder on what they might have already experienced at such a young age and turned her attention toward the back of the plane where a journalist sat typing on his laptop. As with all humanitarian missions, the United Nations allowed a curated reporter and his cameraman to accompany their relief missions and this mission was no different. Except, this time, once the plane touched the ground, no one knew what to expect.

On the far end of the paratroopers were a small group of UN humanitarian civilians; three men and one woman roughly around fifty who looked more like they might have just left the 1969 Woodstock festival. The woman's plump rosy cheeks and red hair hinted that she might be Scottish. Alex was unable to hear anything over the noisy aircraft, but the woman's effervescent personality was evident as she sat talking to the man next to her. They looked like they'd known each other for a long time.

Alex was still deep in thought when the plane shuddered

beneath her and from the corner of her eye she watched as the platoon leader rushed to the front of the plane and disappeared into the cockpit. It wasn't long before he charged back into the cabin area and shouted a string of military commands at the soldiers. Immediately three of his men jumped up and hastily made their way to a palleted crate in the rear end of the plane.

Alex elbowed Sam who had fallen asleep next to her and pushed her chin toward the three soldiers who were busy untying the large crate of army equipment.

Without warning the aircraft suddenly dipped to the left almost causing the three soldiers to lose their balance. Another command ordered three more soldiers who got up and clipped red cords to their waists and the other end to the overhead handrail. The plane tilted sharply to the opposite side and Alex fell forward into her harness causing her oversized ear cups to slip off and slide across the floor. The deafening noise from the aircraft's roaring engines reverberated through her body.

"What's happening?" Alex shouted to the soldier opposite her who stood firm in the centre of the plane; seemingly unnerved by the unsteady aircraft. He ignored her.

"Sit back, Alex. I'm sure it's just routine checks during turbulence. They know what they're doing," Sam called out at her over the noisy engines.

"Something's gone wrong, Sam!" Alex disagreed as she watched the soldiers lock themselves in on the overhead rail and busying themselves with what looked like parachutes. Their faces still displayed emotionless expressions, but their bodies emitted urgency.

Split seconds later there was an explosive sound and the plane lurched first backwards and then sideways. Alex stiffened as she realized they'd lost power in one of the engines. Within moments a piercing siren commanded the remaining soldiers to their feet as, one by one two more men clipped their individual red cords onto the overhead hand rail. Undeterred by the unsteady movement of the aircraft, synchronized to perfection, they pulled their assault rifles across their chests and delivered a sequence of clicking and cocking actions before placing their weapons back into the safety position behind their backs. Waiting for further instructions the combat soldiers stood planted in their places facing the rear end of the plane; a look of pensive determination in their unexpressive eyes.

Alex had enough knowledge of the situation to know that military troops only prepared ammunition when they were readying themselves for combat. She bit her lip. Something was definitely very wrong. She looked back at the two reporters who were also on tenterhooks; now anxiously hanging onto their gadgets and seats. A strong odor of burnt oil and smoke filled the fuselage and Alex found herself tensing her back against the hard surface of the plane. The aircraft quaked violently as if shaken by an invisible hand. The flashing red alarm cast rotating beams of bright red across the silver metal grid floor.

Fear gripped her insides as she tried to take control of the panic that threatened inside her. A clanking noise somewhere beneath the floor had Sam instinctively lift his feet and he pinned his arm across her body. His face was unyielding and now fully engaged in the seriousness of the situation. With her eyes shut Alex curled her arms in a firm clasp around his and tucked her head behind his shoulder. Several more quick successional clanking noises hit the metal under their feet. Panicked shrieks from the Scottish woman echoed through the cabin.

The plane made a sudden drop in altitude lifting its passengers off their seats before turning sharply. Alex tightened her grip on Sam's arm; steadying herself against the plane's sudden change of direction. The commanding officer's deep voice bellowed from the front of the plane.

"Listen up! We are under attack. I repeat. We are under attack. You will be handed a chute and my team will assist you in putting it on. Please remain calm. It is a precautionary measure only. I repeat. Please remain calm!"

Moments later an organized frenzy erupted among the soldiers as parachutes were handed out down the line and passed to the six civilians. The cameraman frantically started taking photos before swinging his heavy television camera over his shoulder.

Before Sam had a chance to stop her Alex had unclipped her seatbelt buckle and pushed her way through the soldiers toward the cockpit.

"Ma'am, please return to your seat and put on your chute," the officer in charge's authoritative voice stopped her.

"I demand to see the captain," Alex shouted over the ear-splitting noise of the aircraft's engines.

"That will not be possible. The captain cannot be disturbed right now, but I assure you all is under control. Please return to — "

"Don't patronize me, Commander. I demand to know what's

happening? What do you mean 'we are under attack'?" Alex argued back.

The commanding officer who was of average height but every bit in charge gripped her arm firmly and pushed her toward one of his men who held up a parachute for her to put on.

"Get your hands off me! I have every right to know what's going on. I demand you take me to your captain this instance!"

The commander ignored her request and instructed the soldier to take her back to her seat.

"Let me go! Get your hands off me!"

"Let her go!" Sam's voice cut across the commotion. Two strides later he pulled Alex from the soldier's grip and walked up to the commanding officer.

"Sir, whilst we have every intention to comply with your instructions, she has the right to know what's going on. Heck, we all do, so I suggest you let us in on what we're facing here."

Sam's towering height was as intimidating as the stern tone of his voice, and it didn't take the commander long to realize that if he wanted to avoid grabbing the attention of the rest of the civilians and reporters on board, he needed to satisfy them with some answers. Chaos midair was best avoided at all cost. He dismissed the soldier and beckoned Alex and Sam closer.

"I apologize, Ma'am, but I need you to put on your parachute immediately. It's for your own safety. It's just a precaution at this stage. Our plane came under open fire as we approached the city. They're preventing us from landing or coming anywhere close to the city's perimeters. One of the bullets hit the number three engine so the captain has diverted off course with the hope of finding a safe place for us to land. Now, I need you to please stay calm, put your parachute on and return to your seat. I assure you everything is under control," and with that, he turned and disappeared into the cockpit behind him before either of them could respond.

Sam hurriedly grabbed the parachute from the nearby soldier and put it on Alex who was still processing the commander's words.

"Let's just do as the man says, Alex. This aircraft is one of the world's best. The Hercules was built for combat and extreme situations. I'm sure it's nothing to worry about."

"Did you hear the part where he said they shot out the engine? SHOT! As in guns shooting at us."

"*One* of the engines Alex. There are four. Extremely powerful ones at that, so we're not going down anytime soon, I assure you."

Sam beckoned a soldier to perform the checks on their parachutes. When they got the all clear, Alex scooped up her earphones from below one of the seats and sat down. She'd expected the mission to be perilous to some extent, but coming under attack this early in the game was not part of the plan. Perhaps this was the precise reason the previous team never made it to the site.

She barely had a moment to compose herself when a loud bang resounded through the air as the plane's right wing took a massive blow. The heavy aircraft shook violently as it wrestled to gain equilibrium.

Several of the soldiers dangled from their red cords and struggled to get back on their feet. Instead of chaos ensuing, the passengers became deadly silence as they watched the paratroopers get back into formation. Miraculously the plane managed to straighten out. The reporter who sat nearest to the window, unclipped his seatbelt and looked out the window.

"Can you see anything?" one of the humanitarians asked.

"Looks like the engine was destroyed. There's too much smoke to be certain but the wing looks intact," the journalist reported.

"So we're down to two engines then?" One of the others shouted across the cabin.

Alex felt her stomach turn as she grasped the accuracy of the relief worker's assessment. The noise levels increased several decibels as the plane continued shuddering. Panic lay across the faces of everyone except the soldiers'.

"How far do you reckon this plane can fly on two engines alone?" Alex spoke in Sam's ear.

"Not sure, but to my knowledge the Hercules is as tough as nails. These planes can take quite a beating before they hit the ground," Sam shouted back.

Alex tugged at her tight harness. The situation made her very uneasy. Across from her the only other female on the plane sat praying; her eyes shut tight and her knuckles white. Alex guessed her to be roughly fifty-five. She wore no make-up and her bright red hair rested disheveled on her shoulders. Alex was pretty certain she had never been in a distressed situation or jumped from a plane before.

It was Sam's turn to be restless. "What do you think the commander is up to in the cockpit? He's been in there a while already."

Contemplating the weight of Sam's question, Alex realized he had a point.

"Where are you going?" Alex shouted after Sam as he jumped to his feet and walked in the direction of the cockpit. She followed, but nothing could have prepared the pair for what they found when they opened the cockpit door.

CHAPTER FIVE

"Commander!" Sam shouted as he rushed toward his unconscious body on the floor.

Tremors ran down Alex's spine as her eyes remained fixed on the two blood drenched bodies of the pilots.

"Sam! Who the heck is flying the plane?"

Leaving the commander's side, Sam leaped over to the first pilot's body that sat pinned down by his seat belt. He was greeted by a bloody mess as half the pilot's face was missing. A rush of air whistled through several bullet holes in the cockpit window.

"He's dead too, Sam," Alex reported as borne out by the number of bullet wounds in the co-pilot's chest confirmed. Frantic thoughts flooded Sam's mind. He looked back at where the commander still lay unconscious on the floor.

"See if you can wake him up, Alex. He's still alive".

Alex knelt at his side and slapped the commander hard across his cheek. "Commander! Wake up! We have a situation." Alex shouted. A second slap across the other cheek made him groan as he slowly regained consciousness.

"What the hell are you doing? You can't fly this plane!" Alex yelled, suddenly aware of Sam taking position behind the wheel.

"Do you have a better idea?" Sam shouted back over the aircraft's noise while clipping the blood drenched seat buckle in position around his torso. Alex climbed over the two dead bodies Sam had piled on top of each other behind the seats and clipped herself into the co-pilot's seat.

"Sam, this is insane! We don't know the first thing about flying a plane. Much less one that is faulty."

A multitude of levers and gauges stared back at her. "How the heck do you switch this thing on?" Referring to the aircraft radio receiver she now held in her hand. Fiddling with the buttons on the panel in front of her she shouted into the mic.

"Mayday, mayday, aircraft in distress. Can anyone hear me, over?"

There was no reply and Alex tried again, switching the dial to the next channel. The plane shuddered and the nose took a sudden dip toward the ground below. Sam's large hands gripped the aircraft's control wheel as he fought to steady the plane. Beads of sweat formed on his temples.

"Come on, come on!" Sam encouraged the plane to respond; his eyes fixed on the artificial horizon indicator on the panel in front of him.

"Mayday, mayday, aircraft in distress. We need assistance. Can anyone hear me, over?" Alex tried again.

The crackling noise of the radio frequency echoed back.

"The comms must be out. It's no use." The commander's strained voice filled the cockpit as he rose from behind holding his hand over his bleeding brow.

"What happened, Commander?" Alex asked with urgency as Sam finally managed to steady the wings of the plane.

"The captain prepared for an emergency landing and the next thing we knew, we were under attack. Last thing I remember was falling back onto the corner of the chair before I blacked out. I guess I was lucky." He glanced at the bodies on the floor.

"Seems you got away with just a grazed brow from the bullet, but I won't be so quick to assume we're going to stay alive here though, Commander. This bird is losing power fast and I'm not sure I can hold her in the air for much longer. We're down to one engine now."

"We're going to have to jump," the commander replied. "I'll summon the men and prepare the civilians. Try to keep it steady if you can. I'll be back."

Alex unclipped her seatbelt and pulled her knife from her boot. With one backward motion she slit the blade through the woven fabric that dangled from the chair.

"Here, let's see if we can tie the steering wheel into position. It won't hold but hopefully we'll have enough time to jump."

"Good idea, climb over and grab the wheel. I'll secure it."

Alex pulled back hard on the wheel. It shook vigorously under her hands draining just about all her strength from her arms.

The commander barged in just as Sam fastened the last knot on the seatbelt around the wheel.

"It's now or never. My troops and the passengers are in position and the ramp has been dropped. We're losing altitude — fast! We don't have a lot of time if we want the chutes to open before we hit terra firma. Have either of you jumped before?"

"Yep, we both have. We're good. Let's go."

Cold air hit their faces as the trio made their way from the cockpit to the cabin where the troops had lined up the reporters and relief team in front of the gaping ramp. From the top of the lowered steel floor, houses and green open spaces moved leisurely below the panicked stares of the relief group.

"I can't do this!" The woman screamed in horror as she stood frozen in front of the gaping fuselage floor. "You can't make me jump! I can't do this!" She screamed.

Alex watched with empathy as the commander entered into an argument over the severity of the situation; resulting in another bout of hysteria.

"I've got it, Commander." Alex intervened, pulling the woman out of line clipping her cord onto the rail in front of her.

"It's ok to be scared," Alex started, gripping the woman hard by her shoulders forcing her to make eye contact. "My first jump was one of the scariest things I have ever done but you can do it. I'll be right behind you. You're much stronger than you think.

Don't dwell on the fear. Just take one big stride and relax. Think of it as the next step in a dance. When it's your turn, don't hesitate or we'll all go down with the plane. The cord will deploy your chute automatically. All you need to do is step out and focus on taking deep breaths. Once the chute opens you take hold of the two levers that will come down above your head. That's what you'll use to balance the chute and steer yourself with. Follow the folk ahead of you and straighten your legs forward and up when you come in for the landing. Got it? You'll be fine."

The woman's bulging eyes from underneath her goggles and fast breathing told Alex that her pep talk had fallen on deaf ears.

"What's your name?" Alex continued in an effort to distract the woman from the situation as the commander performed the last of the safety checks in front of them.

The woman's face relaxed somewhat. "Elaine."

"Elaine, that's a pretty name. I'm Alex and this is Sam. We've got your back, Elaine. You don't have much choice in the matter. It's either you jump or you die with the plane. So which is it?"

Elaine's freckled face went pale as she promptly nodded in acceptance and turned to face her fears.

The commander performed his due diligence on her chute and cord before checking both Alex and Sam's. He proceeded to clip his own cord in at the back of the line behind them.

"Soldiers ready?" he shouted over their heads as his men collectively answered.

"Soldiers ready, Commander."

"Civilians ready?" he shouted again.

"Civilians ready, Commander."

"On my 'go'! Three, Two, One, GO! GO! GO!" the commander shouted propelling the first of his troops to jump followed by the reporter, his cameraman and the three male humanitarians.

"I've got you Elaine, you can do it!" Alex assured the nervous woman when she was three soldiers away from jumping and, much to everyone's surprise, Elaine bravely leaped into the air.

Alex didn't hesitate and jumped immediately after Elaine. Her skin pulled as the force of the air filled her cheeks, threatening to blow her face right off. The air was icy on her skin. Moments later her body jerked up through the air as her parachute opened above her, affecting her breathing for what felt like several minutes as opposed to mere seconds. Once she settled into a steady glide she steered her chute into the direction of the soldiers and the rest of the party beneath her feet. Shrill screams filled the air when adrenalin kicked Elaine's voice into action as her lungs finally filled with air again.

Vast open stretches of farmland steadily drew nearer. Unable to get a clear view of Sam over the cloth canopy above her head, she called up to him after which he promptly hollered back at her.

Relieved, she set her sights on the first soldiers who were due to touch the ground. The thunderous noise of the plane crashing somewhere behind them sent fresh vibrations of terror through her body. A silent conversation with God shifted her mind to once again focus on the soldiers below. Her brief moment of calm dissipated as snapping sounds in quick succession shattered the almost tranquil silence. There was no mistaking it. It was gunfire. Her stomach tensed up as she frantically searched where the bullets were coming from. Another series of gunshots resounded through the air and Alex watched in horror as one of the humanitarian's parachutes collapsed over his head and sent him spiraling to his death. They were all open targets with no means of escaping the fierce rain of bullets that were aimed directly at them. All they could do was pray it miraculously missed their bodies — and parachutes.

As the first soldiers set their feet safely in the middle of a field on a farm below, they executed their tactical combat skills and fired back at the shooters. Elaine's deafening cries echoed through the air as she neared the ground.

"Pull the chords, Elaine!" Alex shouted landing instructions just in time to see Elaine respond to ease her not too graceful landing. It was seconds before Alex touched down alongside an adrenaline pumped Elaine who was tangled underneath the parachute.

"Stay down!" Alex called out urging Elaine to also stretch out onto her stomach underneath the parachute. Squinting against the low beams of the sun, Alex searched the sky for Sam. Her body went numb as her eyes caught sight of his parachute that tilted sideways. When another bullet sliced through the air behind her, forcing her back down on the ground, her breath lodged in a space somewhere between her ribs and her throat. Distraught her eyes searched Sam's chute for bullet holes and found that somehow it was still intact. Realizing he had lost one of his guide ropes she remained fixed on Sam as he fought control over the out of kilter chute. She watched as he floated faster than called for toward the earth. With seconds to go before he was due to hit the ground Alex spotted movement from her right. One of the soldiers ran toward Sam just as he came crashing down and without hesitation, the soldier wedged himself between Sam's body and the ground.

From underneath Elaine's sprawled out chute, Alex stared at the two motionless men that lay on the ground.

"Sam! Are you ok?" Alex yelled across the field as more gunshots flew over their heads. Sam didn't respond.

Taking a chance between the oncoming bullets, Alex crawled on her elbows and stomach toward them through the field of tall yellow grass.

Soft groans escaped the soldier's mouth from underneath Sam's inert body. Alex yanked Sam's goggles off his face.

"Sam! Wake up," she called out with a trembling voice as she tapped both sides of his face and lifted his eyelids apart. He was out cold but still breathing. Her eyes skimmed his body for bullet holes but there were none.

"Sam," she spoke again in a low tone while pulling him gently off the heroic soldier's back. Sam let out a low groan as she pulled him by his arm. He was alive but he had injured his arm. The soldier gently slid out from underneath him, wheezing as he gasped for air.

"You ok?" Alex asked the soldier with concern.

The soldier loosened his helmet's strap below his chin and pushed himself onto his elbows. "I'll be fine Ma'am. How about your friend?"

"I think he's ok, yes. I can't see any bullet wounds."

When the heroic serviceman lifted his head for the first time, Alex spotted he was the young soldier who sat opposite her on the plane.

"Thank you. You saved him," Alex whispered.

CHAPTER SIX

"What's the status, Private?" The commander's deep voice came from behind.

"One comrade and a civilian killed in action, Sir!"

"Who?" The commander responded in a dejected tone.

"One of the relief men, and Murray, Sir."

"Bloody bastards. How many hostiles?"

"Not sure, Sir. I spotted three behind the barn and gunfire from inside the house. We got the civilians out of the line of fire but the female is still unaccounted for Sir."

"Negative. I got her taking cover under her chute over there. She's fine," Alex interjected.

"Ma'am, we need to get you and Dr. Quinn to safety."

"And what about Elaine? We can't just leave her there on her own. I'm pretty sure the adrenaline from her jump has worn off by now. She's in no condition to be left alone. Who knows what she might do?"

"Ma'am, you and Dr. Quinn are our primaries. We got strict orders. We'll come back for her. Now stay down and move as quick as you can."

"I think my arm is broken Commander. I'm going to need some help low crawling across this field."

"We're going to have to make a run for it then. Alex, cover us."

Alex had no time to argue. The commander and his valiant soldier flanked Sam's sides and started running toward the others. The crackling sound of bullets pierced the late afternoon air as soon as they moved through the tall grass. Alex fired her gun at the enemy affording enough time for them to get to safety. The trio ran towards the hay bales, dragging Sam across the field. Elaine let out a high-pitched scream of panic from where she was still lying underneath her cloth canopy. Without a second thought, Alex crawled through the grass to Elaine.

"Let's go!" Alex directed the paranoid woman when the gunfire ceased.

"I'm not moving! I'm staying right here."

"How long, Elaine? Huh? You can't stay here. They know you're hiding under the chute. We need to get to safety. Now, let's go!"

"They killed him," Elaine broke down into sobs. "They killed Geoffrey."

It dawned on Alex that Elaine was referring to the humanitarian who had fallen to his death.

"I'm sorry, Elaine. I'm truly sorry, but I don't think Geoffrey would have wanted you to die along with him. I'm sure he would much rather have you fight back and get home alive. What about your kids and your family back home?" Alex had no way of knowing if she had kids or not, but the clock was ticking and they had to get out of there.

Her wild guess paid off and Elaine wiped her face with the back of her shirt. "You're right, dearie. I signed up for this relief mission and Elaine McDonald always finishes what she starts. What do I do?"

Amused at Elaine's inner resolve, Alex squeezed her hand. "We're going to crawl on our elbows to the bales over there. Whatever you do, do NOT stand up, ok? Stay down and use your knees and feet to push you forward as fast as you can. Ready?"

"Ready," Elaine whispered as she took in a deep breath and crawled alongside Alex to where the rest of the survivors lay behind a large hay silage.

Narrowly escaping the crossfire between their attackers and the defending troops, they managed to safely join their party.

"There's my girl," Sam said with pride as Alex ducked in behind the makeshift barrier taking cover.

Alex smiled with relief to see Sam sitting against the hay. "How are you holding up?"

"I'll live. My wrist is broken though."

But hidden behind their eyes Alex and Sam were fully aware of the repercussions of his injury. With his shooting hand's wrist broken the risk for him to continue with the mission was too great.

"No time for chit-chat kids. Listen up," the commander's voice cut in. "Stay put. I repeat, Miss Hunt. STAY PUT. Out here there's no place for heroics. Clear?"

Alex wasn't sure she liked the commander's sarcasm, but knew she was no longer in charge of this mission and she had no choice but to comply. "Clear Commander."

"Soldiers," he continued. "We counted three behind the barn and unconfirmed hostiles inside the house. Take your mark and infiltrate with caution. Adjust as directed. Miss Hunt, cover us. The rest of you, stay down. Soldiers, on my mark!"

The commander paused to make eye contact with each of his men; communicating a silent language of camaraderie between them as they prepared to attack.

"Advance!" he ordered followed by the soldiers taking up their positions in a synchronized onslaught on their enemy.

Using the hay as a barrier, Alex opened fire at the opposition while the commander and his troops moved in on the farm house. In a frenzied shootout the small army of servicemen skillfully attacked the opposition and in less than fifteen minutes had forced seven hostiles out of hiding and gunned them down.

"Clear!" the first soldier shouted out after which six more

soldiers reported the rivals were obliterated and the coast was clear.

Proceeding with caution, Alex kept her finger on the trigger and her gun in position in front of her chest as she slowly stepped out from behind the hay. Satisfied they were out of danger she turned back.

"You can come out now. We're safe."

"Sir! We have a friendly!" One of the soldiers shouted to the commander as the small group of survivors stepped onto the farm house's porch.

They watched as the commander rushed to where his men had uncovered a small bunker under the kitchen floor and the partially bald head of a man in his late sixties appeared from underneath the floorboards. Clearly shaken by the events the man climbed up the ladder and raised his hands over his head.

"It's ok, sir. We're SADF. Are you the owner of this house?"

Relieved at the introduction of the South African Defense Force the man nodded.

"Are you alone?"

"In the house yes, but my workers live down by the river behind the house."

The commander signaled to four of his men to investigate before continuing his probing.

"What's your name?" The commander proceeded.

"Van, short for Van der Merwe."

Alex pulled out a chair at the modest kitchen table and encouraged Van to sit down.

"Are you hurt anywhere?" she asked.

Van shook his head and gulped down the glass of water the reporter placed in front of him.

"What happened here? Who were these guys?" the reporter cut in.

Van rubbed his forehead and the back of his neck before replying. "This, my friend, is the new South Africa. The free-for-all people taking over this country."

"What did they want?" Sam asked as he shuffled into a chair at the table.

"My farm, what else? It's sanctioned now for anyone to lay claim on any piece of land they so want and who better to steal it from than us farmers. It doesn't matter if my father and his father before him built all this with their own hands. They can waltz in and claim it just because they believe it once might have belonged to their ancestors."

"You mean they buy it off you." The reporter commented for clarification.

Van sat back in his chair and let out a sarcastic laugh. "No friend, you're not listening. They can TAKE it without any compensation, explanation or paper evidence and they can move in with all their wives and all their children and do with it as they please."

"And if you refuse?" Sam asked.

Van repeated his question. "Refuse? There's no such thing as refusing them. They simply kill you and anything that moves and seize your property."

"So you didn't fight back?" Alex asked in surprise.

"Ma'am, even if I fought back and killed them, the government is on their side. I'd be thrown in jail faster than I can get my hat. There are no laws protecting the whites anymore. The government already passed law on land grabbing. Apparently it's their way of punishing us for 'Africa's original sin' as they call it. It's no longer the whites against the blacks in this country. It's the blacks against the whites. You might have won the battle today, but there will be more coming for this piece of land. It's the only one they haven't seized in the area."

The atmosphere in the kitchen lay thick with horror in the wake of Van's declaration.

"Awaiting your orders Sir," one of the onlooking soldiers prompted.

"You're right, Private. Let's secure the perimeter and seal off the entrances."

"Sir, our comms took a bullet. It's out." Another soldier reported as he propped the satellite communications bag on the table in front of them.

"What do you mean out?"

"The Sat phone took a bullet, Sir. I might be able to get a morse code distress out but I'm not sure yet. It will take some time."

Annoyed by the news the commander inspected the bag. "Van, where's the phone?" Turning his attention to the farmer as his eyes searched the room.

"Ha! Phone? You're in the middle of nowhere, my friend. There's no phone lines or internet out here. I suggest you take your vehicle to the nearest town about thirty miles from here — that's if the town is still standing."

Ignoring his sarcasm, the commander summoned his men and went about securing the doors and windows before setting off after the rest of his platoon.

"We parachuted!" Elaine yelled out with a tinge of boasting in her voice.

"Parachuted? You jumped from a plane. Where are you lot from?"

"I'm Elaine, this is Glen and that's Angus. Our friend, Geoffrey didn't make it," briefly pausing before continuing. "We're from Scotland; part of a United Nations relief mission."

"I'm Ethan Reid; WBS News and this is my cameraman Roy. We're with the UN report team."

"And this is Dr. Sam Quinn and I'm Alex Hunt. We're — on the team as well." Alex said with caution as she reminded herself of their mission being classified. "Do you have any medical supplies? Sam's got a broken wrist we need to tend to." Alex continued.

"Down in the bunker," Van got up and proceeded to descend into the bunker. Alex followed.

"What is this place?" She asked as Van switched on his flashlight.

"This is what's kept me safe the last three days. My hide-out."

"Three days! You mean to say they've held you hostage here for three days? What would you have done if we hadn't accidentally come to your rescue?"

"Wait it out, I guess. There's enough here to last me a year."

Alex shone her torchlight across the small underground room's walls. Shelving lined the four walls from top to bottom; stocked with canned food, water and all the essentials a person required to survive. In the one corner was a toilet lid nailed to a rectangular chest; next to it, a small washbowl, soap and some towels.

"It's a compost toilet" Van volunteered as he noticed Alex staring at the contraption with curiosity. "There's a hole in the ground underneath. It's how we did it in the old days. Here, this should do the trick with your friend's wrist until we can get him to a hospital." Van produced a splint and some medical supplies.

"Have you been living here on your own? I mean, where's your wife and kids?" Alex asked with sympathy in her voice.

"My kids managed to find great jobs overseas years ago. My daughter got married and now lives in Germany and the other one is in Canada." Van went quiet and walked towards the ladder.

"And your wife?" Alex pushed causing Van to stop at the foot of the ladder before he turned and replied with a voice filled with heartache. "She died ten years ago — breast cancer."

Instantly Alex regretted her prying. "I'm so sorry. I didn't know."

"No need to apologize, Miss. I think the good Lord knew to spare her all of this. She wouldn't have been able to live apart from her girls, much less live in fear of being murdered."

"Why didn't you leave with your daughters?"

Van, who until now still had one foot on the ladder, turned and faced Alex. "And leave my farm that has been in our family for three generations? Never! I watched my grandfather plough these fields with nothing but an ox and his bare hands and my father after him. We have put centuries of blood, sweat and tears into this farm; worked from sunrise to sunset every day of every year — through wind, rain and thunderstorms. Every crop that has ever come from this land was nurtured and grown by us and our workers who lived and worked alongside us from the very first day my grandfather bought this piece of land. I will die before I ever give up this farm to this nation who now claim they deserve it more than me."

Van's eyes were drenched in an equal blend of sadness and anger; his voice bitter and filled with pride. And without saying another word, he ascended and made his way back into the kitchen.

CHAPTER SEVEN

ICCRU HEADQUARTERS - LONDON

"I'll be damned before I lose another team, General! Find them. I don't care what you do or how you do it, but I need that plane located and fast!"

Matt slammed the receiver back in its place on his desk. Loosening his tie and his shirt's top button he turned to look out the large windows. Rage flooded his tall athletic body as he contemplated the crisis. His hands were clammy on his hips and his heart pounded against his ribs. His inclination to be more active in the field challenged him once again. But against his better judgement he conceded to his board who insisted that he was of more value to their missions being commander in chief from behind his desk. It was at times like these he found himself fighting hard not to exchange his tie for a gun. Perhaps it was his perfectionist nature or being raised as a military brat that he felt the missions would run more smoothly had he been doing them himself. He ran a tight ship and his impeccable ability to always find a way around a problem was one of the reasons ICCRU was so revered in the industry. Matt pulled his tie out from underneath his collar. The thought of failing with this mission strangled his already tight throat. He forced the thought from his mind. It simply wasn't an option. Matt Fletcher was the best in the business.

"Matt, we have a situation," Jean-Pierre DuPont yelled across the room as he barged into his office.

"I know DuPont. We're trying to locate their plane."

"No-no Matt, it's much more serious than that," the French man replied in a hastened tone and shoved a large manila folder against Matt's chest.

"What's this?" Matt replied as he pulled a brown file out from the envelope and moved to the boardroom table.

Red letters on the file marked it as Top Secret. He flipped the bulging file open and skimmed through the pages and several photos.

DuPont was silent as he waited for Matt to catch on to the information he had just given him.

A white rim erupted around Matt's mouth. "Tell me this is a mistake," he said in an emotionless tone through tight lips.

"Unfortunately not."

"You're absolutely certain your Intel is correct?"

"But of course!" DuPont replied with a typical Gallic shrug and French pout.

Matt shut the file with force and paced around his desk.

"Do you realize what this means, DuPont? Bloody hell will this fool stop at nothing?" he vented before continuing. "Do we know why?"

"Apart from feeding his own selfish ego, no. He's a billionaire, Matt. Does he need a reason? Has he ever?"

Matt sat down at his desk and allowed his eyes to take in the detail of DuPont's extensive file. DuPont was right. The man never acted in anyone's best interests but his own. Matt rubbed his hand over the back of his neck and then reached for the intercom.

"Sally, get me the general and patch it through to my secure line please."

Turning his attention back to where DuPont still stood at the boardroom table, he walked around his desk and towered over the small French man. "Who else knows about this?"

"Just us, of course," he said raising the tone of his voice while pulling his shoulders into his typical shrug again.

"Keep it that way, DuPont. We need to keep this under wraps. If word gets out this thing could blow up before we even come close to getting a handle on this. Not to mention jeopardizing the safety of Hunt and the rest of the team. Get as much Intel on him as possible, DuPont. We need to establish his motive and exact location; and cover your tracks. No paper trail, got it?"

"Oui Oui; on it," DuPont replied in French as he left.

Matt moved in behind his desk and slung the folder across the clear glass top. He was angry. Matt Fletcher wasn't a man who failed at anything, much less be defeated by a self-serving Russian billionaire who thought the world was his for the taking. ICCRU had power and influence and hell would freeze over before he allowed Ivan Volkov to exert his demented ambitions over the world.

The sound of his secure line propelled his reflexes into overdrive as he scooped up the receiver on the first ring.

"General?" Pausing for confirmation that it was him before continuing. "Any news?"

"Negative, Matt. There's no sign of the plane and zero response on our communications."

Matt swore under his breath.

"How the hell did this happen, General? I thought we were better prepared this time. Are they even alive? What was their last recorded location?"

"We were as best prepared as we could have been, Matt. May I remind you we're at war here? At this stage we don't know how close they came to landing. We had a distress call come in through a smaller airfield controller. The line was very poor and all he made out was that they were under fire and diverting off course prior to landing. We lost all comms shortly after that. I deployed a ground team but without knowing which direction they diverted to, it's impossible to know where to start our search. It could take months scouting the variables."

Matt shut his eyes in anguish and squeezed the top of his brows under his hand.

"Do we have reason to suspect a crash?"

"There's a distinct possibility, but again, no evidence of it at this stage. It's a waiting game, Matt but Commander Burger and his team are one of the best my army has. If the plane went down, I assure you, they survived it. Miss Hunt's ingenuity isn't to be forgotten either."

The general sensed Matt was holding out on him. "What's really going on, Matt? Is there something I should know?"

Matt glanced at the file on his desk and stared at Ivan Volkov's photograph that had slid out halfway onto his desk.

"We have verified Intel that Ivan Volkov is after the tooth too. We're uncertain of his motives at this stage, but we do know he will stop at nothing to get what he wants."

"Volkov? As in the billionaire from Volkov Industries?"

"One, and only."

"I don't understand. What would an aeronautics engineer want with a fossil?"

"That's the million dollar question. Or in his case, four billion dollars. The man is somewhat infamous for his absurd inventions and theories and let's not forget suspected of being involved with the KGB. If this relic holds any significance to him, Hunt's life is in danger. He's a heartless bastard that goes hard after what he wants. But with his Russian ties we're going to have to tread lightly around this. I don't want the Russian government at our door. I have DuPont seeing what he can dig up, but we need to find Hunt. We can't have Volkov blindside her. They're going to need reinforcements, and General, I don't need to remind you it's classified, right?"

"Affirmative Matt, I'm on it. I'll find them."

A lone with his thoughts Matt studied the folder. Volkov was squeaky clean with a reputation that preceded his brilliance in space engineering. NASA had contracted him on several occasions and it was no secret recent explorations to space and the Mars expedition were mostly accredited to his technology. Volkov Industries defied the ordinary; a clear frontrunner, and their recent success with the launch of an airborne vehicle didn't disappoint. The man was lightyears ahead in research. But Matt held fast to his suspicions that Volkov was dirty underneath his untarnished facade. No one gets in bed with politicians and governments across the world without hiding skeletons in their closet.

Matt's anger turned to annoyance as he failed to find something in the file that would get him closer to knowing why Ivan Volkov would want to get his hands on a three hundred thousand year old fossil's tooth. He was up to something, Matt knew it.

ICCRU had the power and resources of every government agency in the world at its fingertips and if it meant he had to get as dirty as his enemies, then so be it.

CHAPTER EIGHT

"Perimeter is clear Sir and all entrances secured. We found bodies at the river, Sir." The soldier leaned in as he delivered the news in his leader's ear.

"Good job. Take up your posts." Commander Burger instructed his men after which he turned his attention to the civilians who still sat around the kitchen table.

"Van, how many workers did you have?"

Van looked up in horror. "Did? What do you mean *did*?"

The commander cleared his throat. "I'm afraid to say it seems they didn't make it. We found bodies at the river."

Elaine let out an emotional yelp and buried her head in her hands.

"How many?" Van asked.

"Four, one male and three youths."

"No one else?"

"Negative. How many are missing?" the commander continued.

"Just one; Thembi. She's their mother and my housekeeper. She might still be out there. I have to find her." Van pushed himself away from the table and checked the barrel of his rifle before hastily heading towards the door.

"I think it's best you let us handle this Van," the commander stopped him.

Van pulled his shoulders back as he readied himself for an argument but in a brief moment of sanity instantly backed down. He was worn out from hiding in his bunker the past three days and in no physical condition to encounter any foes.

"My men and I will find her. I have two men patrolling outside the house but just to be sure, lock the door behind me and stay alert."

Van nodded and with a heavy heart took up his seat again at the table. Alex, who had just finished splinting Sam's wrist, moved across to lock the door behind the commander.

True to her Scottish roots, Elaine rolled up her sleeves and busied herself with the messy kitchen and a fresh pot of coffee. It was how Elaine MacDonald coped so they let her be.

"Why did you say it was black against white? What did you mean?" Ethan questioned Van.

"It goes back to Apartheid. They just can't move on from that," Van replied.

The reporter looked puzzled. "Care to explain what you're referring to?"

Van shook his head at the reporter's obvious ignorance. "You've never heard of Apartheid? Doesn't surprise me. It seems the world has turned its back on this country; forgetting that Africa opened the gateway to foreign trade. Now we're rubbish, junk status. Forgotten and left to fight it out on our own. Ever heard of Mandela?"

"Of course," Ethan replied. "What about him?"

"Nelson Mandela was supposed to symbolize peace but did you know he wasn't let out of prison because someone proved his innocence? His political crimes were pardoned because he was a pawn in a game far bigger than anyone realized at the time. He marked the end of an era called Apartheid where white and black people were forbidden to live in the same neighborhoods, dine at the same restaurants, frequent the same clubs or share the same public toilets. Total segregation in a white dominant country. Was it just? Of course not! But it was law; set by the then leaders of this country based on decisions they made long before many of today's citizens were even born. And unfortunately not everyone was happy when the ban was lifted; black as well as white. It changed everything and the country's playbook got entirely rewritten. Now, decades later, the scales have tipped and we have an entire generation burdened with hate, unable to forgive; seeking to punish the whites for the past. Contrary to what the world sees, there are an increasing number of whites living in extreme poverty in many of the same conditions as the previously disadvantaged blacks who make the news every day. It goes both ways. Many of us have moved

forward and embraced the changes to legislation and gover-
nance whether we agree with it or not. We're trying to rebuild
this country — together. But fighting against hatred is a
mammoth task so many have given up. Others still fight it and
those who have the ways and means, seek greener pastures. As
for me, I'm stuck here. My children are safe and that's all I care
about but they will have to kill me before I surrender my
heritage."

V an had Alex, Sam, the reporters and volunteers hanging
on his every word as he shared his views when a group of
soldiers banged on the kitchen door to be let it. Amongst them a
badly beaten female held upright by two of the men.

"Thembi!" Van cried out sharply as they carried her into the
kitchen.

Thembi barely had the strength to stand up. Her severely
swollen face made it hard for her to see anything. Dry blood lay
thick on her chin and down the side of her face. Her clothes
were ripped and torn off her body exposing her nakedness in
places. Elaine, who had already caught on that she had been
raped pulled the table cloth from the table and covered her
with it.

"Bastards!" Van exclaimed throwing his chair over as he rose to
his feet and rushed to her side. "What have they done to you?"

"Let's get her in a bath," Elaine instructed Alex. "It might be
best if we get her cleaned up and rested."

Van flew into a rage as the women helped Thembi to the bathroom. "Bastards! I'd kill them with my bare hands if they were still alive!"

"But they're not, Van. You should calm down. She's safe now," the commander cautioned.

"Safe? This is exactly what they do. They rape, murder, plunder and destroy and no one does anything about it. They don't care about skin color! They do whatever the hell they want! Do you know how many of their own women get raped in the back of the taxis and busses on the way to work every day? They're heartless and out of control and Thembi didn't deserve this!"

The commander encouraged Van to sit back down. Van wiped the tears from his eyes.

"Thembi is like a sister to me. Her family sought refuge here when they fled Zimbabwe after the exact same events happened there. Her parents worked this land hand in hand with my father. We've never set ourselves apart because of the differences in our skin color; even during apartheid."

Van paced the room still overcome by anger and sadness when Alex re-entered.

"She'll be ok Van. Elaine's going to take good care of her."

Alex beckoned to the commander to join her in the other room. "Any luck with the comms, Commander?"

"Negative, Miss Hunt. It took too many bullets. The satellite chip took one too. I have my men trying to maintain a frequency to send off a morse code SOS to command but there's no way of knowing how long that will take — or even if we'll be successful at all. In the meantime we're staying put. The perimeter is secured and all entrances barred. "

"Sir, with respect, we're stuck in the middle of nowhere with no comms and as you are well aware I have a mission to complete. Sam's out of action so I have no choice but to go at it alone. I'd like your permission to take two of your men with me, please?"

The commander rubbed his dimpled chin. "Affirmative Miss Hunt. I'll give you Hawk and Smith."

"I'll take Hawk but, if it's ok with you I'd rather take the guy who saved Sam."

"That will be T-bone. He's young and not as experienced as Smith but that boy does have courage. Done. I'll have them ready to deploy at sunrise. In the meantime, we'll try to establish communications with HQ and rendezvous at the heritage site. Agreed?"

"Agreed."

"**H**ave you completely lost your mind, Alex? It's a suicide mission! If our warm welcome here was anything to go by it will be ten times worse out there. You have no idea what you're in for once you leave here and with only two men and no way of staying in contact we might never see you alive again! You should abort the mission, Alex. It's too dangerous."

Alex tightened the laces on her boots and zipped her combat vest up under her chin. She was scared, there was no denying it, but aborting a mission wasn't in her repertoire.

"I can't abort, Sam and you know it. We can't stay cooped up in here forever. Besides, I might find some means to get help. We have no communication with HQ or the outside world and neither you nor any of the relief crew are fit to go at it on foot. I don't see any other way."

Sam knew Alex was already resolved to finishing the mission and nothing he would say or do would deter her from completing it. And unfortunately she made perfect sense. They couldn't stay there forever.

"Where are you heading?"

"Professor Graham's office at the Wits University; it's in the centre of the city. Perhaps he left some clues in his office somewhere. It's a start."

"And how exactly do you intend getting there?"

"Already taken care of Sam. The commander has a map and Thembi gave us instructions on where to find a guy who operates one of the minibus taxis they use. He's about two miles down the road if we cross through the field."

"Taxi? The same taxis Van said they rape women in? Now I know you're insane."

"This guy is above board, Sam. Thembi said he'd get us there safely."

"And you believe her? A taxi driver is going to somehow transport three combat soldiers without a glitch. But of course."

Sam's sarcasm should have angered Alex but instead, it warmed her heart. He loved her deeply and she knew it came from a place of fear and concern for her. She cupped his face in her gloved hands.

"I'll be ok, Sam. Try to rest that wrist of yours. I'll see you when I come back for you."

"Excuse me, Ma'am. Ready when you are," Hawk interrupted.

An hour later Alex, Hawk and T-bone lay camouflaged in the back of a minivan. Jacob was exactly where Thembi said he'd be and the handwritten note she gave them did the trick. But unlike the image Alex had conjured in her mind, the minibus was old and rusted. With sections in the bodywork each clearly belonging to a different color taxi, it looked more like a patchwork throw than a road worthy vehicle. The entire body of the minivan skewed to the one side on its visibly bent axel which made the taxi sway sideways as it started off on the desolate tarred road. The putrid smell underneath the dirty gray blanket forced Alex to flick it off her face a couple of times.

"Down, down!" Jacob shouted back as the van slowed to a halt.

They listened as Jacob exchanged conversation in his native language. From somewhere close by Alex distinguished the mocking and laughing of men followed by torturous groans of someone on the receiving end of some kind of punishment and subsequent loud cheers. It left every hair on her body raised. They dared not move a muscle under the safe protection of the smelly blanket. Unable to see their surroundings or the conditions in which they found themselves, they remained motionless under the blanket. Jacob's easy tone suddenly turned to a loud panicked bawl and seconds later they heard his door open as he was being pulled out of the van. Alex swallowed hard. Her breathing increased and her heart pounded against her chest as she strained to hear what was going on.

"What's happening?" she whispered to T-bone and Hawk who lay equally still on either side of her. Neither replied as they listened to the desperation in Jacob's voice as he pleaded for his life.

"We have to help him," Alex whispered again.

"Stay down, Ma'am," Hawk whispered back, gripping his rifle across his chest.

A split second later the rear door at their feet opened and, as if one man, T-bone and Hawk sat up and opened fire onto the two men who were ready to strike at them with large machetes. Alex jumped over the seats to the front of the van catching sight of several black men whose bodies were ringed by a burning vehicle tyre. The one closest to the front of the van was Jacob. Forced to watch several men bound by a tyre and set on fire alive sickened her. Propelled by a rush of anger she leaped out of the car towards Jacob's anguished cries. Behind her Hawk and T-bone were firing at will against the onslaught of their attackers. The rancid smell of scorched flesh mingled with the strong scent of burning rubber lay thick in the air. A cloud of black smoke covered the victims' bodies as many already lay dead all over the road. Protected by the soldiers' diligent defense, Alex grabbed the blanket from the back of the van and beat down hard against Jacob's body and the burning tyre around his pinned down arms. It made little to no difference to the fire that was being fueled by the gasoline soaked rubber and

Alex watched in horror as Jacob squirmed with pain under the torture.

A moment later Hawk fired a bullet, instantly killing Jacob before grabbing Alex and pulling her back into the minivan. As T-bone sped off with them, leaving an army of corpses in their wake, Alex emptied her stomach contents onto the seat beside her.

"There was nothing we could do for him, Ma'am. He was in agony."

Alex knew Hawk was right. "I know. I've never seen anything like it. Why did they do that to those people?"

"It's genocide, Ma'am. The locals kill off the Zimbabweans. Most of them are illegal in the country; here to work and send money home to their families. The locals are threatened by them. There was no way of avoiding the blockade. They know exactly where to block off the roads Ma'am."

Alex paused as she digested the horrific act of violence she had just witnessed. "I'm Alex, by the way. You can call me Alex."

CHAPTER NINE

The route to the Wits University was burdensome and the trio followed the commander's map in somber silence. On several more occasions they drove past remnants of smoldering bodies in deserted genocide scenes. Other areas displayed burning busses and smashed out shop windows precipitated by loitering. The roads were desolate and eerily quiet with no sign of any life. A few stray dogs wandered the alleyways between once occupied office and residential buildings. Bullet holes and shell casings decorated the walls and streets reminding Alex once again of the treacherous situation she was plunged into.

As they neared the university, distant gunshots catapulted them into full alert.

"Go around the back, Hawk," Alex instructed the soldier behind the wheel.

Burning cars lined the quiet road on either side while piles of furniture lay in ashes in the middle of a clearing. Through clouds of smoke and haze Hawk screeched to a halt as he nearly drove head on into an overturned car that blocked them from going further.

"Let's get out here. We'll enter on foot." Hawk said cautiously, adding for them to check their guns and ammunition.

Several dead bodies of middle-aged men and women laced the narrow garden path to the university's back entrance followed by several more much younger in age. Judging from the gunshots to their backs it was evident they were trying to escape the building. What or who from was yet to be determined. Alex tightened her hand on the trigger and held her aim through the rifle's scope. Hawk entered first, followed by Alex and then T-bone. Books and papers scattered the corridor floor alongside several more perished students.

"It makes no sense. There was no prejudice toward any particular ethnicity. This was a massacre not a racial attack. It doesn't feel right. Something else happened here." Alex remarked as she knelt at the body of a young Chinese male.

"He's still warm. This is fresh. Stay alert gentlemen."

The small team wandered the empty university corridors, alert and ready to fire with nothing but the sound of their footsteps lightly treading the blood smeared polished floors. Hawk signaled with his hand for them to go up to the next floor as they neared a set of stairs. Alex searched the pointer boards on the walls for Professor Graham's office, all the while holding her rifle in position against her shoulder.

When her eyes finally fell on the yellow police tape that lay broken on the floor in front of the professor's office door, Alex knew something more sinister was brewing. Using military signaling, Alex alerted Hawk and T-bone to cover her while she entered. The door stood slightly ajar and no sounds came from within. Satisfied it was safe they entered one by one in trained combat formation. A pool of dried blood on the carpet next to the desk declared the professor's murder scene. With the window blinds slightly closed the spacious room emitted an eeriness that sent shivers down their spines.

"Clear," T-bone called out, followed by Hawk's echo.

"Clear," Alex reported in turn.

"Let's get what we've come here for and get out of here. This place creeps me out." Hawk added as his eyes skimmed over the multitude of fossil bones and skeleton skulls displayed all around the room. In the one corner, pieces of an almost complete skeleton lay flat on a glass table. Next to it stood a few glass cylinders with teeth, bone fragments and vertebrae submerged in lavender colored fluid.

"What is this place?" T-bone asked with curiosity who, up until now had hardly said a word.

Taken by surprise Alex replied.

"These are all excavated fossils of early human species. These ones here date back as much as five hundred thousand years." Alex pointed out a few of the labelled bones.

"I thought we were all apemen. These look human," Hawk added, still wriggling with unease from being in a room full of skeletal bones.

"Many still do. This is exactly the reason why we're here, boys. The professor discovered bones dating back as little as two hundred thousand years ago making it the youngest human evidence to date. This here on the table is Homo *naledi*; your distant cousin and the closest match to our current human species ever found."

"Now that you mention it, I can see the resemblance," Hawk mocked T-bone.

"Focus boys. We're looking for the teeth; the molars to be exact. I'm told the professor hid it somewhere, and judging from his brutal demise, with good reason."

"If he's dead, how sure are we that the murderer didn't take it?" T-bone insightfully queried.

"We're not, but I'm very certain that if someone else had it, it would have been all over the news by now. Something as significant as this can't remain hidden from the world. Even on the black market. I have a hunch his murderer never found it. The professor was too smart and cautious to leave it lying around in his office and judging from the fact that anthropology was his entire life, my guess is he would've died protecting it. Look for hidden drawers or holes in the walls. Somewhere out of sight. It's got to be here somewhere."

The next thirty minutes had the team rummage through the office searching behind the books and under the tables.

"I'm no professional, but this bone seems strange," T-bone commented, handing Alex a femur bone he lifted from the one shelf.

"It's strange because it's not real. The bone is made from rubberized PVC — quite a good replica actually," Alex commented.

"Well done T-bone. You found a rubber bone," Hawk affectionately mocked the young soldier.

Alex ignored the soldiers' friendly banter as she examined the reproduced bone more closely. An accidental twist in opposite directions released a click before the two ends of the bone separated and revealed a paper scroll.

"Found something," Alex informed the two men.

"Well, how about that? Not just a pretty face are you, T-bone?" Hawk jokingly elbowed his comrade.

"It's a rebus puzzle!" Alex said excitedly.

"What's a rebus puzzle?" T-bone asked.

"It's a genius way of hiding a clue by using pictures to represent words or part of words."

"Doesn't look like much to me. Looks like his kid's school art," Hawk commented.

Alex spread the piece of office paper out onto the desk. "Ok, we have a picture of a witch, a heart, a music note and a guy dreaming under a tree."

"That could mean anything. It's a bunch of child drawings."

"It's not, Hawk. I've seen these before. The Egyptians used rebus puzzles all the time. Each picture translates into a word and the full word is usually the name of a place. Once we find the place we need to go there to either find the teeth or another clue. We just have to play around with it."

"This could take forever," Hawk said with frustration as he moved across to the window and peered through the blinds.

"Like Pictionary?" T-bone added, ignoring Hawk's obvious irritation.

"Indeed. Let's take the picture of the witch. It could literally spell out part of a word or sound similar to one." Alex paced the room as she sounded off possible option. "Itch, pitch, switch, it, pit, wit, wits! That's it, Wits. We're here, at the Wits University. That must be it. What's the next picture?"

"A heart," T-bone added with excitement.

"A heart; let me see. Heart, cart, dart, smart..."

"Fart?" Hawk blurted out from where he stood guard at the door.

"Don't be an idiot, Hawk," T-bone bit back in embarrassment over his team mate's crudeness.

Alex was too submerged in her own thoughts to notice their childish squabble as she searched for the correct answer. "Maybe something to do with love? Wits love, Wits heart..."

"Maybe Wits art?" T-bone ventured.

"Wits art; could be. Heart, art — I think you might be onto something T-bone, well done. Maybe there's an art room some-where in here. Let's go," Alex beckoned tucking the scroll down her shirt.

"Don't we need the rest of the puzzle?" T-bone asked again with obvious enthusiasm over the guessing game but Alex was already halfway down the corridor.

"Come genius, I have a feeling there will be more for you to decipher," Hawk nudged as he set off after Alex.

T-bone watched as Hawk disappeared around the corner after Alex. Seconds later gunshots spat through the corridor having T-bone duck into the nearest doorway. With both Alex and Hawk out of his vision there was no telling where the shots came from or if either of them got shot. The gunshots ceased and he waited before cautiously popping his head out for a visual of the corridor. With his finger on the trigger he ventured into the empty passageway and paused at the corner where Alex and Hawk disappeared. His heart thumped against his chest. Straining his ears for any sounds or movement he swallowed and leaned his head out and back from behind the corner. T-bone caught his breath as his rapid tactic resulted in a clear visual of Hawk lying parallel to the floor and the side stance of a man holding a knife to Alex's throat. Adrenaline rushed through his body as he leaned out again for another look. There were two more hostiles in a well-lit laboratory slightly ahead of them. T-bone considered his next move. With Hawk down and Alex at knifepoint, he was outnumbered against the three men so attacking them from behind would trap Alex in a crossfire. He peered down the other end of the long corridor that continued beyond the entrance to theirs. If he jumped across and continued further down the corridor he might get lucky and surprise them from the other end. Deciding this was his only option, T-bone took a deep breath and darted across to the other end of the passageway hoping he was fast enough not to be detected by any of them. Satisfied that they were unaware of his presence he proceeded with caution as he made his way down the passage. With his back against the wall T-bone paused briefly before turning up into the next corridor. Relief flooded his body as his gamble paid off and he seemed to have success-fully navigated his way in a precise square around the perps. His new positioning had him perfectly lined up for Alex to spot him; opening the opportunity for a coordinated surprise attack on the men. But if he leaned out around the corner, even just enough for her to see, it risked her captor seeing him too. Annoyed at being snared in a deadlock, T-bone searched around for another option. His eye caught sight of an air duct above his head. With newfound vigor he decided to risk it. A man of average height he was just tall enough to slip his fingers through the bottom end of the grid. The steel framework lifted away with ease and seconds later, T-bone had successfully maneuvered his body through the opening. He cursed inwardly as the rubber from his boots scraped against the steel walls of the duct, causing an amplified screeching noise. He stopped, anticipating that he had alerted the gunmen. Relieved that they hadn't heard him, he took a slower pace and proceeded with caution. It was hot and sweat trickled over his brows into his eyes. Crawling on his knees with only one hand while the other gripped his rifle was no easy task but he knew he was within close proximity to them. The sudden audible voice of Alex's keeper confirmed his assumption as it echoed through the duct. Paused in position at the vent opening directly above Alex and her captor, T-bone allowed his eyes to examine the position of the other two men in the lab's doorway. Dressed in blue suits and armed to the elbows, T-bone deduced they had to be a private security team.

"Who are you?" Alex demanded an answer from the two men.

"That is none of your business." Another male voice answered back jerking T-bone's attention into full alert. He had underestimated the number of attackers. There was someone else in the lab.

"It most certainly is my business if I've got a knife against my throat and am held hostage by your baboon over here." Alex shouted back as she tried to wrestle her way out of her keeper's tight grip.

"You're hardly in a position to question me woman. I think the more important question is who are *you* and what are you doing here?"

Alex didn't answer.

"So, we have ourselves a tough one here, guys? A little Miss GI Jane it seems." The man held Alex up in ridicule. "Well, Miss Jane, you're not going to live long enough to tell this tale in any event so I'll bite and play this ridiculous little game of yours. You're looking at the man who will rule the new world and blow all the pathetic little people left on this one to hell."

His arrogant words left Alex cold and she swallowed hard against the sharp blade on her neck. From above T-bone listened as the faceless man's footsteps sounded through the lab.

CHAPTER TEN

"Find that tooth! I don't care what you burn down or who you kill but I want that tooth!" The steely tone of the man's voice instructed his posse. His words were harsh and heartless. Anger flooded her trembling body as Alex watched him walk up to her.

"Ever wonder what the world would have been like if we never left the Garden of Eden, Miss Jane? Wouldn't it be extraordinary to have a brand new world free from contamination, war and strife? A utopia, so to speak with pre-engineered humans who lived in perfect harmony with each other. Wouldn't you rather have paradise than this?" Waving his hands around the room.

"*This* isn't all that bad. It's bad people like you who mess it all up," Alex snapped back.

"Bad? You think I'm a bad person? Well, then you clearly don't know who I am, Miss Jane. Ever heard of Ivan Volkov?" The man said smugly.

Alex felt her jaw tighten as the introduction left her feeling numb in disbelief. She knew exactly who Ivan Volkov was — multi-billionaire inventor extraordinaire who had just executed the first successful mission to Mars. The same Ivan Volkov whose billion-dollar tech lab manufactured groundbreaking neuron-activated prosthetics and was on the brink of finding a cure to cancer. The man was a walking saint.

"Ah, I see you have heard of me then," Ivan smiled as Alex's eyes revealed her thoughts. "I have the power to do whatever the hell I want, and extracting the mitochondrial DNA from this latest find is exactly what I need to build myself a new Garden of Eden. A perfect paradise with perfect humans. My very own creation in my very own new world. But enough about me and all my power, I'm betting your name isn't really GI Jane."

Ivan waved his hand at the man behind Alex to release the knife around her throat. Alex exhaled quietly when her attacker removed the knife.

"Now then, let's try this again. Who are you and what are you doing here?" Ivan pushed.

The attacker pulled the cable tie firmer around Alex's bound hands reminding her of her vulnerability.

"Alex," she replied through tight lips.

"That wasn't so hard now was it? Judging from your British accent and combat attire you're not here for a holiday. Why are you here?"

Alex had her back up against the wall, but declaring her hand would expose the entire mission. Her keeper pushed his gun hard into her ribs.

"Official university business and as for my outfit, it's the latest fashion."

Ivan bellowed a deep sarcastic laugh. "Careful, Alex, you don't want to mess with me. You mean nothing to me. The only reason you're still alive is because I sense there's more to it than what you're letting on. Not to mention of course that I hate being surprised. So you will be collateral for now until I figure out what you're really doing here."

Ivan Volkov turned on his heels and walked back into the laboratory where a small team of scientists were busy transporting test tubes to a large biohazard suitcase. "Lock her up in the back," he shouted over his shoulder.

Alex glanced back at Hawk's dead body on the floor behind her. T-bone was nowhere in sight which meant he was still alive. A fleeting thought to make a run for it was quickly quelled when her ribs took another hard shoving of her keeper's gun.

The small storeroom in the back of the laboratory painted an equally dismal picture with no windows to escape through. The bodies of two university scientists lay in the middle of the floor. Alex wriggled her wrists in a futile attempt to free her hands but the cable tie was too tight — even for her small hands to slide through. She had her hunting knife hidden in her boot around her ankle but there was no possible way she could reach it with her hands bound behind her back.

Her eyes scanned the contents of the room for any sharp objects to cut through the restraint. There was nothing but folders and plastic bottles of chemicals. A single glass vial with a plastic daisy stared back at her from the bookshelf. That would work but breaking it would make too much noise and alert them. Unable to grab it with her hands she used her mouth and slowly lifted it off its wooden base. The vial tasted dusty on her tongue. She looked at the bodies on the floor. Making use of the shelf against her back she sat down against it and used her feet to push the two bodies next to each other. Maneuvering the furthest body to act as a stopper, she pushed the one closest to her on its side and then leaned over to drop the small glass container on the floor beneath it. The corpse provided the perfect sound barrier as Alex pushed down hard onto the vial. The muffled sound of breaking glass told her the plan worked and she quickly slid a piece of glass up and down against the plastic cuff around her wrist. It took some doing but before long her wrists were freed.

Propping her ear up against the door she heard Volkov talking to the scientists. Her hands might be free but she was a long way from escaping. With that being the only way out all she could do was wait until they were gone.

"Psst," a whisper came from above her head and Alex found her looking up at the ceiling into T-bone's welcoming eyes.

"You're a genius T-bone," she whispered back, impressed at his ingenuity to have lifted one of the ceiling panels.

Alex reached up but was too short. With their fingertips barely touching it was impossible to gain a firm grip on his outstretched hands. She gently tugged at the bookshelves which proved far too flimsy to hold her weight without falling over. Her eyes skimmed the two bodies on the floor. Alex pulled the smaller of the two on top of the other and carefully climbed on. The improvised step produced the exact amount of height. She tried not to ponder on the disrespect toward the deceased scientists under her feet and whispered apologies at them. With her body raised it allowed enough height for T-bone to wrap his hands around her wrists and pull her up through the roof.

"Am I happy to see you," Alex whispered as T-bone slid the ceiling panel back in place; covering the trail.

"Come, this way." T-bone led Alex across the rafters and through a maze of air ducts until the pair found themselves escaping through the back of the building. Their feet thumped on the tarmac as they ran toward their dilapidated minibus.

T-bone jumped in behind the wheel taking a moment before starting the engine. "Hawk's dead."

"I know. I'm so sorry. We ran straight into Volkov's men. He didn't stand a chance against them. Are you ok?"

T-bone nodded and sped off. "Who's this Volkov guy anyway?"

"You don't know? He's probably the most loved man in the world; everyone's Mother Theresa. A real wolf in sheep's clothing he turned out to be. If only they knew what he was up to."

"Yeah I couldn't quite make that part out from where I was. What exactly is he up to?"

"He's a psychopath. Yes, he managed to build a shuttle that flew to Mars and back but the genius has it in his mind to create his own paradise of pre-engineered humans and take over the world."

"Did you say create humans?" T-bone asked confused.

"Yup, the very tooth we're after contains a unique strain that traces us back to Eve. It's called the mitochondrial gene. Somehow scientists have figured out a way to extract this gene and according to Volkov, he can use it to create his own humans. I guess he wants to play God."

"So he wants to clone us?"

"For lack of a better word I suppose. We know China just successfully engineered a new species of monkey so I guess it's entirely possible."

"Well, then we need to find that tooth before he does, Ma'am. Whereto next?"

Alex pulled the puzzle out from her shirt, grateful Volkov's men never searched her. "Ok, let's assume we've correctly cracked the first two images — Wits and Art. The next image is a music note. What could that be?" Alex mumbled to herself. "Music. I can't think of any words that rhyme with music. Wits Art... I think it is safe to say the university isn't quite where one would have art, right? So perhaps we're looking for another venue altogether?"

T-bone frowned. "Your questions are rhetorical correct? I mean it's not like I know what you're talking about."

Alex smiled. "Where's the map?"

T-bone pulled the map out from where Hawk left it in the driver's door. From the corner of his eye he observed Alex studying the map all the while still mumbling the clues to herself. "Wits Art Music Dream... Wits Art Music Dream. Got it! Wits Art Museum. The music note is the first two letters of Mu-seum and the dream rhymes with 'seum'. Get it? That's it. Let's go, it's not far from here."

T-bone shook his head in disbelief. "I can't believe you figured that one out."

"Years of experience and the two best mentors in the world, T-bone. What's your real name, by the way? I'm sure your parents didn't really name you after a piece of steak."

"No Ma'am, it's Ezra. I have a birthmark on my collar bone that resembles a T. So the guys in the squad started calling me T-bone."

"Well, nice to meet you Ezra. Please stop calling me Ma'am. My name is Alex, short for Alexandra. I think we've long passed the formal titles."

A lex and Ezra navigated the streets of Johannesburg with caution. By now Volkov would have discovered her gone and, after declaring his deranged plans, would certainly stop at nothing to find and kill her. He had a squeaky clean reputation and exposing him for who he truly was would undoubtedly lead to his demise. But right now, exposing Ivan Volkov as a fraud wasn't her top priority. Yes, they needed to watch their backs, but finding that tooth was her mission and the only thing occupying her mind.

Nearing the centre of the city, Alex and Ezra proceeded with extreme caution. The streets were eerily quiet; as if everyone had just picked up and left. Passing a street of houses they noticed the residents peering out from behind the curtains. The doors and windows were shut, barricaded from the outside with wooden planks nailed across the frames.

"So that's where everyone is; hiding inside their houses," Ezra commented.

A loud thumping noise against the rear window caught Alex and Ezra by surprise. Several more banging noises on the back of the van and along the sides caused Ezra to drive faster. Out of nowhere a group of young men jumped in front of the car and flung firebombs at the front window. Fueled by unsolicited anger and hate the gang shouted phrases of profanity at them.

"Drive Ezra!" Alex directed reaching for the windscreen wipers to squirt water on the flaming wiper blades.

Ezra pushed his foot hard on the pedal, knocking one of them over. Both Alex and Ezra cringed in silence as the wheels lifted and drove over the gang member's body. The unavoidable act increased the gang's fury sending one of them into a shooting frenzy. Six bullets hit the minibus's back door. Ezra sped off and turned the corner, avoiding the possibility of getting their tires blown out. They'd stand little to no chance fighting off an enraged gang of eight on their own. But, while they had managed to get away from the gang behind them, the pair had driven directly into another group of violent youths beating a middle-aged white man with baseball bats in the middle of the street in front of them.

Ezra stepped hard on the brakes sending the van's rear end into a screeching forty-five degree angle stalling the engine. The stationary position of the minibus left them trapped and exposed across the street. On the one side, the angered gang came running around the corner and on the other side, they came face to face with the violent youths beating up the resident.

Without a second thought Alex climbed between the seats and flung the van's panel door open. Two of the four youths charged at her with a baseball bat and a hockey stick. She grabbed the first one by the arm and flung him up against the doorpost causing him to become disorientated. She yanked his baseball bat from his hand and whacked it hard against his back leaving him to fall unconscious to the ground. The second youth flung his hockey stick at Alex's head. She ducked and punched the baseball bat into his stomach. Incapacitated and gasping for air, he fell to his knees in pain. Ezra's frantic attempts at starting the engine again finally succeeded. With two of the four youths down the other two cowardly ran away leaving the badly beaten man curled up on the street.

"Get in!" Alex shouted and pulled the injured man into the van before ordering Ezra to step on it.

Twenty seconds later they turned three more corners and were in the clear.

CHAPTER ELEVEN

"It's ok, you're safe now. I'm Alex."

The injured man lay stretched out across the row of seats in the minivan. Still crouched in pain from the violent beating he forced his swollen eyes open; silently thanking Alex for saving him.

"Here, have some water," Alex offered. "Do you live nearby?"

He nodded.

"Where's your family?" Alex continued.

The injured man gulped down several sips of water. Finally able to breath normally he sat up and answered in a strained voice.

"Back there; at my house. They're locked in the basement."

"What were you doing out in the streets? They nearly killed you," Ezra cut in.

"I was trying to get home from work when they attacked my car."

"What exactly is going on? Why are people hiding in their houses? I mean it doesn't appear to be racial? We've just come from the university and found victims across all ethnicities."

"It isn't about the color of your skin anymore, Alex. It's a war between political parties; a struggle for power. Unfortunately there are thirteen different parties all believing they know what's best for the citizens and this country. But if you ask me, none of them have a clue what they're doing."

"And the civil outbreak? Why isn't the government stopping this?"

"Things didn't go down too well after the recent presidential election. Before we knew it we had a coup on our hands and well, things got out of hand and people took matters into their own hands. I don't see it ending unless the parties reach a peace treaty. And to complicate matters even further, there are about eleven different cultures all fighting for their own ancestral rights. It's a mess."

The man paused and stared at Ezra's reflection in the rearview mirror. "Which side are you on?" he directed a question at Ezra; a hint of hate in his voice.

Alex cocked her head to one side. "What do you mean 'which side is he on'?"

"He's colored. He can't be both."

Ezra felt the cold sting of the man's harsh words. He had never thought of himself being of any color. All he ever wanted to do was fight for what's right; regardless of race, faith or creed.

"Does it matter?" Alex said sternly while climbing back into the front seat next to Ezra. "He saved my life and indirectly yours."

She glanced at Ezra's stern face. Hurt stung behind his brown eyes. She didn't know anything about him, but what she had come to discover already was that Ezra was a man of courage and strength.

Alex looked back at the man they had just saved. "You can't come with us. We're going to drop you off at the church up ahead. You should be safe there."

Ezra found the church icon on the map in his lap and set off toward it.

"I see how it is. You've obviously hooked up with the guy. Seems a bit young for you, but hey, to each its own, right?"

Alex stiffened at the man's shameless accusations. If she were the heartless human being he clearly was, she'd deliver him back to that gang for a well-deserved beating.

"Stop the van, Ezra. I think he can find his own way from here."

Alex pulled her gun from her holster and pointed it at the man's face. "Get out," she ordered in an emotionless tone.

"You can't leave me here. I won't make five yards down the road. They'll kill me!"

"Perhaps they should. Now get out." Alex beckoned with the gun.

Ezra leaned out his window and opened the sliding door from the outside. "You heard the lady."

"Assholes! You're going to regret this!"

As soon as he stepped out Ezra sped off leaving clouds of exhaust smoke in his face.

"You ok?" Alex whispered as she took her seat next to him again.

"I've had this all my life, Alex. Nothing I'm not used to by now. But I am sorry you got dragged into it."

"I'm a woman, Ezra. Most men forget we were put on this earth for purposes other than sex. He's an ungrateful, chauvinistic pig who got what he deserved. We, on the other hand, have a mission to complete. So let's get on with it, shall we? The museum isn't far from here."

I t came as a surprise when, contrary to the rest of the city, the museum wasn't desecrated. With the extensive glass panel doors perfectly intact and locked, the pair stood out front and contemplated their entry.

"We can't draw attention by setting off the alarm," Alex commented as she traced the keypad lock with her fingers. "There has to be a freight elevator around the back."

The back of the glass building seemed undisturbed and they quickly climbed the high security gate with ease. Empty pet bowls warned the possible presence of guard dogs, but closer inspection revealed none.

"Another deserted building," Ezra remarked. "There," pointing to the freight elevator obscured by a delivery truck.

Alex pounded the button with her fist. The door remained closed. Her eyes scoured their surroundings and found a steel bar sticking out from underneath a wood pallet.

"Help me," she instructed Ezra who promptly wedged the rod between the elevator doors. Alex's fingers strained against the tight crevice in an attempt to pull the doors apart. Their efforts paid off and the doors sprung open; revealing a gaping shaft dropping two floors down. Alex looked up into the shaft. The elevator was stationary one floor above their heads. Wasting no time, she leaped onto the suspended cable and made her way up to the elevator floor above her head. Ezra followed as soon as she had navigated her way into the narrow space between the lift and the wall. It took all of three knee extensions before she was on top of the elevator's roof. With Ezra now next to her they unlatched the roof panel and dropped down into the lift. The doors parted with ease under their combined pulling effort and they soon found themselves in the foyer of the art museum.

"What are we looking for?" Ezra asked as he took in the enormous open space.

"Not sure, but I would imagine it to be something relating to the professor's field of study. He was a paleoanthropologist so let's see if we can find an exhibition correlating to this."

"A paleo what?" Ezra said puzzled, having no idea what that meant.

"Anything to do with ancient human history. Human skulls,

fossils et cetera. Essentially anything you think might belong in his office."

The museum displayed various paintings and African statues, clay art, beading and several African masks but nothing remotely related to human bones.

"Nothing here," Ezra yelled back from the opposite side of the considerably sized hall.

"Nothing here either," Alex called back spotting the circular ramp along the outer walls. "Let's go up to the next floor."

The sloping surface spiraled up to the next level and Alex and Ezra found themselves side by side in another exhibition hall. A multitude of glass boxes containing animal bones, human bones and rock art decorated the floors and walls.

"Something like this maybe?" Ezra asked as he pointed to a display cupboard with three drawers.

Alex joined his side as he stood over an opened drawer exhibiting three apelike skulls on a bed of beach sand. They were replicas of Homosapien skull fossils, each with a separate scientific name tag and explanation.

"Yup, that will do," Alex answered lifting the first one up to inspect it more closely. She read the label tag out loud.

Homo erectus

About 1.75 million years ago

This hominid has a number of similarities to early Homo erectus including an exceptionally small cranium, rounded occiput and face similar to KNM-ER 1814. The presence of this specimen in Dmanisi, Georgia suggests that the first humans to disperse from Africa had smaller brain cases than Homo erectus.

"Remarkable. What does the second one say?" Alex asked Ezra as she put the first skull back in its place.

"Nothing like that. If I'm honest I can't quite make ass or elbows of it. But I suppose that's science for you."

Ezra placed the skull replica back in its place and proceeded to pick up the next one in the tray.

Alex leaned in to read the tag on the second skull.

Homo habitis

About 2.5 million years ago

The windows of his soul delivers the call where Homo's ancestors introduced Dewey to Decimal. Between jackets and spines lie the hidden root that reveals to all the submerged foot.

She paused and read it again. "You're right. It doesn't sound like the other one." Alex read it again, this time slower. Her pulse quickened and her mouth broke into a wide grin. "It's a clue, Ezra! It's a clue!"

"It looks like a crushed skull that had been patched together with putty. Are you sure?" Ezra queried scratching the back of his neck.

"Absolutely, we just need to figure it out. '*The windows of his soul delivers the call'*. That's obviously referring to his eyes, or in this case the cavities."

Alex stuck her fingers into the empty holes where the eyes once were.

"And? Can you find something?" Ezra nudged.

Alex pulled her flashlight from the pouch in her vest and shone it into the skull. Straining her eyes to get a visual she gasped with excitement as she spotted the sequence of numbers.

"It's numbers; 927.381"

"That's it? Just six numbers. It's too short for a mobile number as the clue suggests." Ezra threw out a theory.

Alex read the clue again "Where Homo's ancestors introduced Dewey to Decimal. Between jackets and spines lie the hidden root... Wait! Dewey to Decimal. It's the Library! Of course! Between jackets and spines. Get it? Books. The libraries organize books according to the Dewey Decimal system. The first three letters reference the particular broad subject, like science, literature et cetera, while the second three numbers indicate the sub-section of that subject. We're looking for a book in the library. Let's go!"

Alex dropped the skull back into the drawer and started running toward the elevator.

"Wait! What about the root and submerged foot part? What does that mean?" Ezra yelled after her as she sped down the ramp.

"Not sure yet, but we'll figure it out."

Ezra laughed under his breath as he followed hastily after her. He had never been part of a treasure hunt and this excited him to no end.

Back at the minivan, Alex spread the map open on the dashboard. "Do you have any idea which library it might be?"

"I've only ever come to one library and it's the Johannesburg City Library. It's a couple of blocks away."

"That's a start; certainly seems like the most logical. Let's go."

Alex pulled her seatbelt across her chest and glanced at Ezra as they took off. She never noticed that he was of mixed race. It didn't matter much to her, but she was curious to know more about him. "Were you born in Johannesburg?" She asked cautiously.

Ezra's eyes met hers briefly as he turned the corner. "Nope, Cape Town."

His voice was tainted with a somberness Alex didn't quite understand.

"So your parents still live there then?" Alex probed further in an effort to lighten the mood. Instead, her question prompted Ezra's lips to tighten into a thin line. He looked away without answering.

"Sorry, I was just trying to get to know you."

Ezra's shoulders tensed up as he cleared his throat. "My parents are both dead, Alex. My mother was killed by a revengeful white farmer on the day Mandela was released, and my father died shortly after the army called me to service."

Alex drew in a sharp breath. "I'm so sorry, Ezra. I had no right to ask." She watched as his knuckles turned white on the steering wheel. The cold tone of his voice spoke volumes about a lifetime of hurt. Deciding to focus her attention on the map instead, she sat quietly in her seat.

"I was barely five at the time. I watched them shoot my mother in front of the whole world and no one did anything about it. Yes, she was black and my father white, but she didn't deserve to die."

"No one does, Ezra. It's ok to be angry."

"That's just it Alex, I'm not. I've moved on and yet here I am; serving the country and expected to kill the very people who killed my mother. How can I? I understand the concept of defending my country against foreign enemies, except I'm not though, am I? We're caught in the middle of a self-inflicted war. A war between this country's very own people. And for what? Power? To prove a point? No one can change the past. It happened. Why can't this country move forward?"

Alex listened as Ezra's voice changed from sadness to anger and then despair. "I can't answer that, Ezra, but I do know that you're one of the bravest souls I've ever met, and if you could overcome such a horrific act of hatred, then anyone can."

Ezra shuffled uncomfortably in his seat as his eyes caught sight of the only other car in the street from his rearview mirror.

"I hate to spoil the moment, Alex, but I think we have company."

CHAPTER TWELVE

"It's Volkov. We can't let him find out we're heading to the library. Do you think you can lose him?"

"I'll try," Ezra replied as he pushed his foot down on the accelerator, dodging a charred couch in the middle of the street. The taxi van expelled clouds of black smoke from the exhaust pipe as Ezra accelerated. Moments later a loud clanging noise filled their ears.

"I think we just lost the exhaust."

Alex turned to look out the rear window. "Affirmative, we're going to need to change vehicles. We're about a block away from the library. Turn here." She instructed Ezra who promptly turned the vehicle into the opposite direction in an attempt to lose Volkov. It didn't work. With the exhaust gone, the minivan was losing power — and with that their head start.

"There!" Alex pointed to a parking garage up ahead. "Hopefully we might gain enough distance between us to allow time for us to abandon the car and find another one."

The basement parking was dark and totally deserted. A few overhead lights flickered, emitting orange sparks every couple of seconds. Ezra maneuvered the van around the garage, increasing speed on the straights. It took three more corners before he headed up the ramp, bouncing over a metal studded speed bump. Alex had her head turned to face the back, expecting Volkov to come around the corner, but remarkably they had successfully managed to gain enough distance to have lost sight of them.

"Pull in under the ramp," she directed Ezra who screeched the van in a hundred and eighty degree circle and pulled in underneath the ramp; wedging the roof between the cramped overhead concrete space. The tight positioning prevented either of their doors from opening. "Out the back!" Alex yelled already climbing over the rows of seats to the boot. The dilapidated state of the vehicle proved in their favor as it only took one kick for the rear door to open and they fell to the ground. The screeching sound of car wheels around the corner warned them that Volkov had caught up and they rolled underneath the row of abandoned cars to the left of the van. Obscured by the darkness and wall angle, Volkov's car sped past and up the ramp to the next level.

Alex and Ezra crawled out from underneath the cars and bolted for the stairwell.

"Hurry, they'll figure out we dodged them somehow," Alex yelled as they barged through the stairwell door of the floor below. Her eyes searched for a car that would be easy enough to hot wire.

"I got this," Ezra declared and Alex watched as the young

soldier shoved his elbow through the window of a nearby car and climbed in. A mere second later the engine started without a key even before Alex had a chance to shut her door properly.

"I'm impressed," she remarked.

"Yeah don't ask. I did a lot of stupid things when I was a kid."

The gray sedan navigated the corners far easier than their previous mode of transportation and shortly after they had already reached the parking garage exit. Alex glanced back. "Looks like we lost them. Well done Ezra."

"Shall we chance it to the library?"

Alex nodded as Ezra gathered speed the moment they exited the parking garage. A split second later bullets hit their vehicle's roof, catching them both by surprise. Bullets slammed into Alex's door and behind her seat the window shattered into a million pieces.

"Damn it! Now they know what car we're in," Ezra swore.

"They have a bird's eye view from up there so go around. If they see we're heading for the library they'll come for us there."

Ezra took a sharp left and another sudden right turn; disappearing between a row of tall office buildings. In that moment of safety Alex felt the sharp pain in her shoulder and reached to rub it. When she pulled her hand away from her arm she felt the sticky wetness between her fingers.

"You got shot!" Ezra expelled as he noticed the blood on her palm.

"I'm fine. We need to get as close to the library as we can and go the rest on foot before they find the car. Park up in that alleyway."

Still concerned with her injury, Ezra did as she instructed and hid the car in a narrow street between the buildings. Blood seeped from Alex's arm leaving tiny droplets on the paving. Ezra searched the car and found a shopping bag with linen in the boot. Relieved he ripped one of the sheets and tightened the expensive cotton rag around her bleeding arm.

"That should do for now. We need to make a run for it," Ezra voiced as he fastened the last knot. Aware they were now an open target for insurgent groups, they readied their guns and set off down the street. The sudden sound of men's voices coming from the entrance to a nearby block of flats alerted them and they ducked behind a garbage bin. Alex searched for another way through. Turning back wasn't an option. Blood had started to seep through the bandage and she felt lightheaded.

"This way," Ezra whispered as he pulled Alex to her feet and opened a rusted metal door behind them. The door shut loudly behind them and Ezra cursed at his negligence. Convinced it had alerted the gang to their presence, he pushed the leg of a nearby broken barstool across the door handle. It wouldn't hold but it might buy them some much needed time. Behind the door it was dark and they realized they had come through the back entrance of a street club. Old cigarette smoke hung thick in the air. The sharp acid stench of old urine stung their nostrils when they ran past the toilets. The loud banging of the metal door behind them warned them that their suspicions were correct and the gang had caught up with them. Alex pushed away the frantic wave of fear that engulfed her body, which was now weakening under her straining legs. Dozens of dead bodies lay strewn across the bar floor. Many of them already decomposed and it took nearly everything for Alex not to expel her stomach contents. Ezra paused briefly at the green stained-glass front door before he flung it open and stuck his gun out. Alex followed suit. Their path was clear and they bolted down the street. Ezra pulled Alex by the arm around the corner just as they heard the bar door bang behind them. With any luck they had turned the corner just in time. Oxygen pumped vigorously through her veins as Alex pushed her body to the extreme. She was no longer in control of her legs which seemed to give way with every step she took. Her temples throbbed and her mouth was dry.

"Almost there, Alex."

Alex was aware of Ezra's comforting voice moments before everything went black.

The soothing warmth of a damp cloth against her forehead brought Alex back to consciousness. Her lips stuck together as she tried to open her mouth to speak.

"Shh dear, just rest."

Her eyelids were heavy and the room spun fiercely when she heard a woman's shrill voice pierce her aching head.

"Ez, bring your aunty some water!"

Confused, Alex forced her eyes open to see a short, overweight black woman seated next to her.

"Where am I?" Alex murmured confused. "Where are my clothes?" Suddenly aware she was in her underwear under a blanket.

"Hey, you're awake. Shh, it's ok. We're at my aunt's house. We're ok. Here, drink some water."

Alex leaned her head forward to take a drink of water from the glass Ezra held up against her lips.

"What happened?" Alex whispered.

"You passed out while we were running away from the gang. It must have been the bullet wound. You lost a lot of blood."

Alex recalled the gunshot to her shoulder and instinctively reached for it. Her fingers slid across a fresh bandage.

"My uncle is a vet. He managed to remove the bullet while you were out."

"A vet?" Alex panicked.

"Yes, yes, desperate times call for desperate measures. It's the same procedure so you were in good hands, don't worry. You might start barking like a dog soon though."

Alex smiled at Ezra's silly attempt to make her feel better.

"You need to eat some soup, dear," the shrill voice of Ezra's aunt cut in. "My mother used to say nothing fixes you up faster than homemade chicken soup."

"This is my aunt Nozipho. We call her Aunty Nozi for short," Ezra introduced them.

"How long have I been out?"

"Not that long; about eight hours. It has given us enough time to evade Volkov and the gang. There's no way he'll find us here."

Alex searched the room. "Where are my clothes? We need to get to the library."

"Not so fast, you're still recovering. My uncle gave you a strong sedative. Besides, it's almost midnight. Eat your soup and sleep it off. We'll head out tomorrow morning first thing."

There was no reason to fight it. Ezra was right. She hardly had enough energy to lift her hand to feed herself, much less run away from Volkov.

The sun peered through the small single window in Aunty Nozi's kitchen. Her house was entirely made from corrugated tin sheets and the size of an oversized garden shed. Against the one wall a tin bowl stood next to a kettle, a toaster and a two plate stove. Against the opposite wall was the single bed Alex had slept in and a small chocolate brown couch pushed up against the third wall. As tiny and cramped as it was, it was as neat as a pin and evident Ezra's aunt took great pride in her humble abode.

"Eat dearie, you need to build up your strength." Aunt Nozi placed a breakfast bowl with steaming brown sludge in front of her on the table. Alex stared at the runny chocolate colored goop in her bowl.

"It's porridge. We call it Maltabella — made from malt. Here, add some sugar and milk," Ezra explained as he added a sprinkle of white sugar and a dollop of milk.

As non-appetizing as it appeared, Alex was starving. The instant strength after the first spoonful was welcoming and she found herself tucking in with fervor. Ezra smiled in the knowledge that no one had ever been able to resist his Aunt Nozi's famous porridge.

W hen they stepped through Aunt Nozi's front door, Alex was instantly greeted by several boisterous black kids who clung to Ezra's legs. They ranged between the ages of five and eleven and beamed with happiness. Their joy was infectious and simultaneously admirable. Even though their clothes were either several sizes too big for them or several sizes too small, and they were all barefoot, they had not a single care in the world. Bubbling with life they followed Ezra as he led Alex through the bustling township. Once at the edge of the community of patched shacks, Ezra handed each of the kids a lollipop and a handful of candy. "Off you go now. It's time for school," he added as they skipped happily off down the path.

"They're not mine just in case you wondered."

Alex smiled. "You'd make a great dad though."

"Maybe one day when all this is over. Come, I have a friend

who found us a new car. We're a solid twenty minutes from the library. I'd say we get on with it."

And true to his friend's promise, they found their transportation parked and ready under a nearby tree. Looking every bit like a drug lord's car which clearly didn't belong in a rural settlement such as this, Alex dared not ask where the shiny black Mercedes came from. The less she knew the better and when Ezra threw his hands in the air communicating a silent 'don't ask', her suspicions were confirmed.

CHAPTER THIRTEEN

The tranquility of the abandoned road leading out of the township was short lived. Alex and Ezra realized anew that the country was still very much at war when the road ahead was blocked off by an oversized fuel truck. Throwing caution to the wind, Ezra slowed down well in advance but didn't stop. He knew these tactics all too well. This was a country whose people now played by their own rules. Alex shuffled nervously in her seat when Ezra cocked his gun in his lap. "What's wrong?" She asked as she followed his lead and took her gun off safety.

"See the shadows moving behind the truck's wheels?"

Alex nodded.

"We got ourselves some hijackers. They force you to slow down and then they pounce on you."

"To do what exactly?"

"Whatever the hell they want. They're mostly after the cars and any valuables like mobile phones or laptops. If you don't cooperate they kill you."

"How many do you think there are?"

"Hard to say but I'd guess at least four."

"And I suppose that opening to the side of the tanker was intentionally created as a trap," referring to the makeshift drive-through on the one end of the truck.

"You guessed it," Ezra confirmed.

Alex turned back to look behind their car. "Can we turn back and go another route?"

"We could but it's a hell of a detour around the city. I'd say at least a three hour drive; and that's if we don't run into any deterrents."

"Well, then I reckon we fight them off." Alex said as she climbed to the back seat.

"I guess now will be a good time to see what your friend gifted us with," unzipping a khaki duffle bag to reveal a small arsenal of curated weapons.

"I suppose I don't need to ask if these are legit," clicking the magazine of a sniper rifle in place. "I'm pretty sure this is a government issue SSG-69. Let's see if this baby delivers. Hold it steady, Ezra." Alex instructed as she pointed the barrel through the space below the passenger seat's headrest.

"Ready?" she checked.

"Ready," Ezra answered.

Alex shot a clear round hole through the glass that left the entire front window intact. With sniper precision the bullet hit her target and the first hijacker fell over from behind the wheel. A split second later, Alex fired off the next bullet and another body fell flat to the ground. All hell broke loose as an army of six more hijackers retaliated. Crouching down behind the steering wheel and the dashboard, Ezra drove the car directly towards the truck and pulled the handbrake, spinning the car's rear wheels parallel to the stationary fuel truck. Alex had switched positions and guns and fired a succession of shots from an automatic machine gun through the rear passenger window. One of her bullets grazed the tarmac and sparked a pool of fuel that had leaked onto the road from the fuel truck.

"It's going to blow, Ezra! Go, go, go!" Alex yelled for Ezra to drive through the hijackers' decoy lane around the truck.

The Mercedes' tires spun pale gray smoke into the air as Ezra turned the car towards the open lane and sped through seconds before they felt the explosion's powerful impact from behind.

"Hahaa! That was the coolest thing I've ever seen!" Ezra cheered displaying every bit of his young age as he caught sight of the fuel truck exploding in his rearview mirror. "Remind me not to mess with you."

Alex smiled climbing back into the passenger seat next to him. "Let's just hope your friend wasn't planning on getting his car back," she commented while she knocked her gun's handle against the remaining pieces of broken glass in the window.

"I'm pretty sure he won't since it wasn't his in the first place," Ezra laughed. "And with any luck this episode was the last hindrance and we can finally get to that library now. I'm curious to see how this treasure hunt plays out. Who knows? Once we have that tooth in our hands I might just have a reason to leave the army and join you."

"I can only hope you will, Ezra."

And as if the universe heard their pleas, the rest of the trip was smooth sailing and fifteen minutes later, they parked the car a street away from the Johannesburg City Library's front entrance. Evidence of vandalism from the night before still smoldered on the steps to the front door. Bookshelves and mounds of half burnt books greeted them as they walked toward the entrance. Alex tried to control the nerves that gnawed away at her insides as she squatted down next to the ashes.

"Let's hope the book we're after isn't amongst these."

Unlike the museum's doors that were firmly locked, the library's doors stood wide open. A stray cat darted past their feet from inside the doorway. Alex tightened her sweaty hands around her handgun's grip and aimed the weapon at the space in front of her face. Synchronized in silence the pair moved back to back through the front door; alert and ready to shoot. The sudden noise of a bird frightened off its perched position in the roof trusses, heightened their senses. Relieved it was just a couple of pigeons they slowly continued through the foyer. They appeared to be alone but nothing on this mission so far had come without surprises. Continuing in full alert, they climbed over the steel turnstiles and proceeded through to the enormous room of books. Tall bookshelves, overturned in some places, deposited scattered books across the royal blue carpeted floors. Above their heads the galleries that stretched out from the walls looked undisturbed. A final check confirmed they were indeed alone and Alex bolted away from Ezra towards the bookshelf closest to her.

"What are we looking for exactly?" Ezra whispered.

"A book, with the numbers 927.381 on the spine."

Alex dashed from shelf to shelf as her eyes worked through the numbers on each row of books. Ezra did the same on the opposite end.

"My numbers are all in the three hundreds," he called out.

"Keep looking. I'm positive it's a book."

Several minutes passed as the two ran from shelf to shelf.

"There have to be a million books here, Alex. How sure are you we're actually looking for a book?"

"Oh it's a book, Ezra. Trust me. I spent half my life in libraries. Keep looking."

"I'd listen to Miss Hunt if I were you."

Volkov's obnoxious voice echoed through the library. Caught completely off guard Alex took cover behind the bookshelf. A sudden overwhelming sensation of dread took over her mind. She closed her eyes and took a deep breath. She was aware Ezra had also ducked behind one of the shelves in front of her but there was no way of telling where Volkov was.

She swallowed in a futile attempt to slow down her rapid breathing as she waited for Volkov to speak again.

"It took my men all night tracing your steps. Miss Alex Hunt; renowned relic hunter. Yes, I now know exactly who you are and what it is you're after. It appears we're after the same thing."

Alex strained her ears trying to establish his position over the hollow echoes of the library. She detected shuffling of feet somewhere behind her. She slid her back along the bookshelf down to the floor taking up a squatting position and held her gun up against her nose. Her fingers flexed around the trigger and she carefully popped her head around the shelf in both directions. The shelves behind her delivered no one and she leaned her head back in position against the wood barricade. A drop of sweat trickled down her brow. She squeezed her eyes shut to help it along.

"Why don't you and your young South African soldier surrender, Alex? I could do with your skills on my team. I'd certainly pay you far more than the pittance you're earning at the moment. You and I would make a formidable team, don't you think? You can be part of something much bigger and more important than finding ridiculous lost treasures. Help me find that tooth and I'd not only let you live, but I'll let you enjoy the splendor of my very own paradise; my very own Garden of Eden. This tooth is the only piece missing, Alex, so if you think I'm going to let you steal my piece of paradise, you've got something else coming. One way or another, I'm going to create a new human race, Alex; with or without you. No man on this planet can offer you what I am offering you right now so I suggest you consider it carefully."

Alex swallowed uncomfortably as disgust pushed its way up into her throat. The man was clearly deranged. But, as much as Alex wanted to believe his mission was impossible, she also knew Ivan Volkov not only had the money, he also had the power and influence to make anything happen.

Hell would freeze over before she would play a part in his twisted game of pretending to be God. She had to do something. Five shelves ahead of her Ezra poked his head around the shelf and spotted her. He signaled that he suspected two of Volkov's men were on top of the overhead gallery, confirming her hiding place was bound to be exposed if they carried on walking. Alex signaled back that she was going to make a run for it. She took a deep breath and bolted for the wall, disappearing in the shadowy safety under the overhanging gallery. From her position under a row of desks, she saw Volkov's shiny black shoes slowly pacing the aisle toward Ezra. Crawling on her hands and knees under the tables she came back within Ezra's vision and warned him of the impending danger. Ezra's eyes widened but she held up her palm for him to wait. She needed a distraction to lure Volkov's men out and away from Ezra. She closed her eyes searching her mind for ideas. In the distance the pigeons cooed at the entrance. If only there was a way of frightening them it could create the distraction they needed. Her eyes frantically searched for some-thing to throw toward the birds. Apart from the books, there was really nothing else that would travel the distance while going unnoticed through the air. Annoyed she moved her gun from one hand to the other and then she froze. A bullet; she'd use a bullet.

With resurrected vigor she pulled a bullet from her vest pocket and crawled across the floor, taking up a new vantage point behind a cupboard. Aware of Volkov's men still pacing the gallery above her head, she flung the bullet through the air in the direction of the perched birds. Much to her surprise her launch was flawless and the pigeons squealed in frenzied mayhem through the air. Alex disappeared under the desks and watched as her distraction lured Volkov and all four of his cronies out from their hiding places. Seizing the opportunity Ezra ran toward Alex and together they disappeared through an office door.

CHAPTER FOURTEEN

Once inside, the presumed office revealed the library's large archive room. Ten narrow walkways divided the floor to ceiling steel shelves that displayed dozens of old books, folders and sealed filing boxes.

"Here," Alex whispered to Ezra, standing at the bottom of an antique-like spiral staircase located in one of the dark corners at the back of the room. Skipping every second step, they leaped up the hand carved wooden stairs that eventually delivered them inside an even darker, cramped loft office. In the centre of the much smaller room stood an oversized wooden desk encrusted in a thick layer of dust and piles of leather-bound books. It smelled like an attic and appeared to have been out of use for years. Unable to see much, Alex flicked on the small desk lamp and picked up one of the brown leather-wrapped books. She drew in a sharp breath. "These books are signed first editions, some of them dating back a hundred and thirty years. They must be worth a small fortune!"

"Alex, have a look at this one!" Ezra excitedly let out and pointed to one in particular.

Unlike the other books which clearly hadn't been used or moved in years, he handed her one that was entirely free from dust as if it were left there the day before. The brown leather-bound book was covered with gold embossed rock paintings and a scarlet silk ribbon ran through the middle of the book's pages.

Alex turned the book over. Her eyes widened at the sight of the digits on the spine which read 927.381. A tingling sensation in her chest engulfed her as she pulled at the ribbon and flipped the book open.

"Is this what I think it is?" Ezra whispered over her shoulder.

"Uh-huh," was all Alex managed to utter as she flipped through the book's pages.

"So now what? What are we looking for? Wasn't there something about a foot in the riddle?"

Alex quoted the rest of the riddle from the museum's index card.

Between jackets and spines lie the hidden root that reveals to all the submerged foot.

"Yup, that's the one. Now I hate to be the one to crash this party, Alex but we should really get out of here. Your bird decoy won't hold them off for much longer," Ezra added.

Ezra hovered at the top of the spiral stairs. The office below was quiet but Volkov was a smart man. He looked around to see if there was another way out and marked the hatch in the ceiling above his head.

"This might be our only way out Alex. Bring the book. We have to get out of here now!"

Alex nodded in agreement. She shoved the book into her pants' waistline in the small of her back and covered it with her black combat vest. Ezra was tall enough to lift the hatch off with ease.

"Get on," holding out his interlocked palms for Alex to step onto. She did and Ezra lifted her up through the hatch into the safety of the roof.

"Hurry," Alex whispered for Ezra to pull himself up. He did so effortlessly seconds before they heard the office door below open up. Replacing the door to the roof hatch, Alex and Ezra moved quietly from rafter to rafter in the direction of the front of the building. They trod lightly, hoping the narrow roof trusses would remain sound under their weight. Several rats scurried away under their feet as they manoeuvred the tight, dark space in the library building's roof. A few paces away they noticed a beam of light cutting through the darkness to reveal an illuminated area not far from where they were.

Alex led the way to find an air duct skylight pushing out onto the roof. The duct's metal hinges were bolted to the roof trusses. Alex reached for her Swiss knife in her pants and flicked the screwdriver attachment into place. With the sun sitting higher by the minute the roof was hot and uncomfortable and it took several minutes to loosen each screw. But eventually the hinges came apart and they lifted the metal rectangular box away from the roof. Alex managed to squeeze her body through easily, but

Ezra's shoulders were too broad; even at a sideways angle. Alex lay on top of the angled roof that was slippery with years of piled on dirt. She dug her combat boots down hard onto the black clay tiles and yanked four roof tiles off from around the duct cavity until the space was big enough for Ezra to climb through.

Positioned halfway up against the side of the pitched roof it was steep and slippery.

"We need to climb up to the ridge. We'll get a better footing there," Alex suggested and managed to easily pull herself up to the ridge. Once there they hung their legs over the sides as if on a horse and lifted themselves across the ridge to the nearby valley of the roof. Alex didn't hesitate and slid her body down along the valley to where she landed feet first on a flat stretch of the roof. Ezra followed. Relieved the roof opened up to a fair strip of leveled surface, they ran across to where it abruptly stopped dead at the back of the building. In front of their feet was a sheer drop to the street below delivering a gaping space between the library and the neighboring building's roof.

Behind them they heard Volkov's men ripping up more roof tiles around the air duct. Alex eyeballed the distance to the next building. "Do you think we can jump across?"

Ezra looked back and then across to the next building's flat roof. "Not sure. We'd need a hell of a runway to leap this far."

"Is there another way?" Alex asked stretching her head over the side of the roof in search of a fire escape. There was none.

The announcement of Volkov's men on the roof's ridge behind them sent shockwaves down her spine.

"I guess we have no choice now, do we?" Alex alerted Ezra. The pair hastily walked backwards until they were satisfied the runway's distance would be sufficient to propel them over the gaping space between the two buildings.

A last reassuring visual exchange triggered Alex and Ezra into a full sprint across the flat roof. Adrenaline surged through their veins, forcing every bit of oxygen from their lungs as they both leaped through the air. Deafened by the sound of their thudding heartbeats, a brief moment of weightlessness possessed their bodies; ensued by the undeniable piercing sound of open gunfire. Alex was aware of Ezra's feet successfully hitting the roof in front of her as her body thrashed into the edge of the building. Piercing pain stung her hands as she gripped the sharp edges of the brick with her fingers. The blow against her ribs knocked her wind out and she gulped for air. A bullet hit the brick next to her, missing her head by mere inches before she felt Ezra's strong hands around her wrists.

"Use your feet, Alex!" He shouted with a strained voice.

Alex was numb with fear as she clung for dear life off the side of the building. She clutched onto the sleeves of Ezra's jacket and fixed her eyes firmly on his. Another bullet narrowly missed her arm.

"Push Alex!" Ezra yelled.

Alex dug the front of her shoes into the wall and pushed hard while Ezra pulled her onto the flat roof next to him. Several more bullets hissed over their heads as the pair stumbled to their feet. Volkov's men had gained on them and opened full fire from the library roof behind them. Still attempting to get up to run,

Alex felt a stabbing pain in her knee that forced her flat on her face again. Adrenaline pushed through Ezra's battle seasoned body when he leaned back for her. His hands seized her arm and he managed to pull her petite body into an upright position. Finally back on her feet, fighting the pain from her injured knee, Alex ran toward a nearby external ventilation shaft as fast as her legs could carry her. Engulfed by dread she felt the weight of the leather book lift away from the small of her back and drop onto the roof floor behind her.

A bullet narrowly missed her foot in the split second she paused. Ahead of her Ezra had safely reached an external ventilation shaft and ducked in behind it. Now sheltered by the metal walls of the vent Ezra fired off several shots at Volkov's men; affording Alex a brief moment to go back for the book.

Chancing it, she reached back only to have to side-dodge a new bombardment of bullets. The quick reflex movement forced her body on its side, grazing her cheek across the coarse roofing. Vulnerable and exposed she instantly got back onto her feet and scooped the book up. Ezra fired off several more shots. Using every technique she had acquired during her recent military training, Alex tucked into a combat roll and safely took up cover next to Ezra. With the book firmly stuffed down the front of her shirt and snug behind her combat vest, Alex took a desperate deep breath while she looked for a way. She searched the fringes of the building as much as her obscured vision allowed while Ezra continued shooting at the men. They didn't have much time before they'd be ambushed so escaping through the building was no longer a viable plan.

"Cover me!" She yelled as she bolted across to the other end of the roof and ducked behind an octagonal cupola. The tightness in her chest lifted when she spotted the fire escape down the side of the building.

"Ezra over here! I'll cover you!"

He responded the moment Alex took over and started shooting at Volkov's men awarding Ezra exactly enough time to run safely from his position to where she sat crouched behind the cupola. With their bodies just about fully shielded by the eight protruding corners of the dome-like roof structure, they were now at a safe angle and out of the opposing line of fire. Running the risk of being surprised by their attackers via the building's roof exit, and with no time to waste, Alex pulled Ezra by the arm and yelled, "Let's go!"

Already heading over the edge of the building and down the narrow steel ladder that sat mounted to the side of the building, Alex descended followed closely by Ezra.

When their feet safely touched down on the asphalt street at the bottom of the ladder, their fear slowly subsided in the knowledge that their car was parked just around the next corner and that they had managed to once again, escape Volkov.

Now, out of danger from the fierce onslaught of Volkov's men and with their fleeing position still undetected, the pair bolted down the quiet street toward their car.

CHAPTER FIFTEEN

"That was touch and go Alex! Who the hell are these guys?" Ezra said as they got into their car and sped off aimlessly down the street away from the library.

"One seriously deranged man if you ask me. I have to find a way to make contact with ICCRU. We might not be this lucky next time. I have to let them know who this man really is. Just in case —"

Ezra's eyes briefly left the road to look at Alex. "In case what? We die? That is not an option Alex. We're going to complete this mission and you're going to get on a plane back to the UK with that tooth in your hand. Agreed?"

Alex wiped a tear that threatened to run down her cheek. The liquid soothed her badly lacerated fingers. She had been in many dangerous situations since doing this job full time, but nothing quite as challenging as this one. And, as nice a partner as Ezra was, she missed Sam more than anything. If she died and never saw him again, it would be a torturous death. She swallowed hard, forcing the lump in her throat down. She couldn't let that happen. She'd have to do whatever it took to get back to the only man she had ever loved.

"How do you do this, Ezra? Fighting in wars every day of your life not knowing if you'll ever make it home? You have your entire life ahead of you. Why not choose to marry and have kids and take up a normal job?"

Ezra went quiet. His knuckles sat white around the steering wheel. With a voice drenched in sadness, he answered her.

"I was only four when I watched my mother get killed in front of my eyes. Shot dead. She didn't die from a heart attack or cancer or a car accident, but because she was black. Because the white man behind us thought the color of his skin somehow qualified him to be superior to her. It was the day Nelson Mandela was freed and apartheid abolished. It was supposed to be a new beginning for our family and the entire country. Instead, it caused even more segregation. And here I am. Caught in the middle — neither black nor white. I see how the white people are brutally murdered and chased out of their companies and off their land, just like Van experienced. And equally so, I understand why the black people hold so much hatred and animosity toward the whites. So where do I fit in? Which side of this racial fence am I supposed to sit on? My father was white and my mother black and all their lives they were forced to live separately; separate churches, separate schools, separate restaurants. Heck even when they were married they couldn't be seen together. Their entire marriage was a secret. I have just as much reason to be angry at the white man who murdered my mother as the black men who invaded

Van's house and took what wasn't theirs. But two wrongs don't make a right. So I fight back the only way I know how. I fight for what's right — equality, respect, peace. I have no home. Just a conscience and a dream to see this country united. I want all blacks and whites to put the past behind them and move on. Forgive and start new. That's why I do this."

Alex sat in silence and found herself staring at Ezra. Though only in his early twenties, he was wise beyond his years. The day she saw him opposite her on the plane she knew that he was different, and what she saw today displayed every bit of the courage and wisdom she spotted in his eyes that day. Ezra's courage gave her exactly what she needed to complete this mission — a cause worthy of fighting for.

"We need to stop this lunatic from getting his hands on that tooth," Alex declared with newfound motivation.

Ezra pulled the car over on the side of the road. They were far enough outside the city but without knowing where they'd be heading to next, it seemed smarter to save their fuel.

"So the next part of the riddle from the art museum said something about a foot that will show us the route, right? What does the book say?" Ezra asked.

Alex recalled the second part to the riddle and said it out loud as she took the book out from underneath her shirt and flipped it open to where the bright red thread ran between the pages.

Between jackets and spines lie the hidden root that reveals to all the submerged foot.

"Seems there should be a map of some sorts showing the route then. We got the book part. We just have to figure out the hidden route that will reveal the submerged foot," Ezra said again.

"Not exactly, it was spelled r-o-o-t and not r-o-u-t-e," Alex corrected him.

"We're looking for the root of a plant then," an excited Ezra guessed again feeling every bit the part of a relic hunter's sidekick.

He leaned in to look at the open book on Alex's lap who had gone very quiet all of a sudden.

"The pages are empty. There's nothing there. The entire book is blank. I don't understand," Ezra exclaimed with irritation.

Alex skimmed over the open pages. "Well, one thing's for sure. The professor certainly had enough foresight to make sure the tooth stayed protected. He made certain it wouldn't be found that easily."

"Now what? We're in the middle of Johannesburg with no idea where to find a hidden root or whose foot is under water. It's a wild goose chase!" Ezra vented to which Alex responded with a giggle.

"If there's one thing I've learned my friend, then it's to never take anything at face value. There's always a clue. You just need to know what to look for."

"I see a book with blank pages. Not to mention we have a

psychopath on our trail. I might have courage but chasing after rainbows is not quite my thing."

Alex flipped the pages back and forth and then back to where the red satin thread marked the book. She lifted the book to her nose and smelled the pages.

"Mothballs right?" Ezra said with sarcasm.

"Nope. Lemons."

"Lemons! Now there's a new twist on the phrase 'when life gives you lemons you make lemonade,'" Ezra mumbled with a pinched expression on his face.

"Our clever professor used one of the world's oldest methods to conceal a clue. A method used by pirates and kings alike."

"Ok you've lost me, Alex. I have no idea what you're talking about," Ezra said throwing his hands in the air.

Alex got out of the car and walked to a clearing in the brush behind the car.

"We need to make a fire," she said hastily collecting some twigs and piling them on top of each other.

"You're going to burn the book?"

"No silly, the professor wrote the clue in lemon juice. When you heat the pages up from underneath it creates a chemical reaction that reveals the clue. I only need a small flame."

"Will a lighter do?" Ezra took a gold Zippo lighter from his pocket and flicked it open. "It's my good luck charm. It was my dad's."

Alex grinned "Now isn't that good luck indeed! That most certainly will do the trick."

"So how do we do this?" Ezra asked; happy to have redeemed himself.

"Just move the flame underneath the page starting from the top down. Not too near the pages though. We don't want to burn a hole in it. We need just enough heat to react with the lemon juice," Alex directed.

Ezra did so with caution and much to his surprise, Alex's theory proved accurate as he watched the outlines of a map magically reveal itself.

"Do you recognize this place?" Alex asked.

"I think it's the — zoo? It's a map of the zoo. Why would he send us to the zoo?" Ezra queried.

"There, it's a picture of a gorilla in a cage with an X marking the spot. Perfect!" Alex yelled; her facing beaming as she got back into the car. "Let's go!"

"Go where? The Zoo?"

"Yup, our professor hid the next clue in the primates' enclosure. Oh that's genius. Get it? Primates... evolution, he hid it with the gorillas. He definitely had a great sense of humor that's certain."

"You can't be serious. When was the last time you saw a gorilla? Do you realize they can tear us apart? And who's to say the zoo is still standing? We could be walking into a deathtrap with wild animals all over the place."

"I once spent several days in the open Savannah and came face to face with lions on more than one occasion, Ezra. We'll be fine. Promise."

The Johannesburg zoo wasn't far and as predicted by Ezra, they were greeted by a fierce eagle hovering thirty inches tall over a cape cobra. When Alex and Ezra came closer the bird fanned his wings in the air and let out a high-pitched whistling sound. Ezra held his arm out in front of Alex. "It's an Eagle and that's his prey. I'd steer clear if I were you."

"Well, he's blocking the entrance and we don't have all day."

Alex picked up a piece of a broken brick that lay behind her on the pavement and tossed it toward the snake. The snake struck at the brick affording the Eagle the perfect opportunity to seize the moment. He snapped his sharp beak around the snake's neck and gripped the cobra with his sharp talons. Seconds later the powerful bird took flight to a nearby tree with his dinner in his mouth.

"Come," Alex pushed through the revolving gate.

Barely inside the zoo a single gunshot hit the metal gate behind them and Alex and Ezra ducked sideways behind the ticket office to take cover. The unexpected strike left Alex cold; her heart racing as her fingers closed over her gun.

"Can't be Volkov's men," Ezra whispered; equally shocked by the surprise attack. "There's no way they followed us," he continued.

Taking cover Alex slipped in through the ticket office's door and rummaged through the desk drawers. Her fingers found a cracked compact mirror. Using it to get a better visual on the entrance gate she held it sideways through the small money slot. Ezra was right. It wasn't Volkov. She crawled back to where Ezra sat in hiding behind the wall. Her movement sparked another attempt at killing her followed by loud jovial applause.

"It's a gang; clearly out to play games and cause trouble."

"How many?" Ezra questioned.

"Not sure, I only saw three. Their faces are covered with bandanas and they have revolvers. Looks like a bunch of kids."

"Kids using us for target practice or a gang initiation," Ezra commented. "The city is full of these gangs. They're amateurs though. I say we shoot back to show them we're armed. Hopefully it will scare them off enough to move on."

Alex nodded in agreement and crawled back into the ticket booth. She pointed the barrel of her gun through the slot and fired two bullets at the youths' toes.

"Idiots," Ezra mumbled under his breath as he watched them run away.

"Right, now that's out the way, where do you think the gorilla enclosure is?" Alex asked as she set off down the narrow path.

"Careful Alex, I'm pretty sure the eagle and its prey weren't the only animals out of their cages."

"With any luck the gorilla's out of his enclosure too then we can slip in and out and move on."

The map led them down a winding path which stopped in front of a twenty foot enclosure. Inside, a large male gorilla paced the fence while a female and her weak infant sat under a large tree. They were trapped inside and it was evident they hadn't eaten for a while. The male made loud grunting noises. He was aggressive and not likely to allow anyone in at this stage.

"If we can distract them with food it might give us a chance to get inside." Alex suggested.

"Are we sure the clue is here?"

Alex ignored Ezra's dubious question and disappeared through a doorway behind the enclosure.

Minutes later she dragged a large container out the door and in front of the gorilla's cage.

"Ever fed a gorilla?" Alex teased. "Today is your lucky day Ezra."

CHAPTER SIXTEEN

BACK AT THE FARM

"Sir, we have company," a soldier interrupted Commander Burger from where he was fiddling with the satellite equipment at the large dining table.

"How many? What are their positions?" He fired off two questions as he abruptly got up and cocked the gun in his hand.

"We're not a hundred percent certain but it seems we're outnumbered Sir. There are at least eight in the field behind the house and we spotted about ten more hostiles out front. They're approaching fast."

"Get the squad in position." The commander walked over to where Sam sat playing a game of cards with Ethan and Roy in the sitting room.

"We have company guys. Arm up, we're going to need all hands on deck if we're going to survive this attack."

Sam and the two reporters promptly did as ordered and followed the commander into the kitchen.

"Do you have any more weapons in the house Van?"

Van, who was having a cup of coffee with Elaine at the kitchen table, startled at the commander's sudden entrance and spilled his coffee across the tabletop.

"You bet. Follow me," leading the commander down into the bunker.

"What's going on dearies?" Elaine asked anxiously as they all gathered around the table.

"We have some untimely visitors. It's perhaps best you and Thembi take shelter in the basement. You'd be safe there. Come, hurry!" Sam pulled Elaine up by her arm where she sat frozen at the table and nudged the two females toward the bunker.

"Where are Angus and Glen?" The commander asked upon his return plonking a large brown trunk on the kitchen table.

"I think they were playing a game of chess in the study. I'll go get them," Roy volunteered.

"Do we know how many there are?" Sam asked as he watched the commander unpack the arsenal from the trunk onto the table.

"We're surrounded. My men reported at least twenty hostiles along the perimeter of the house. There's no time to waste, they're closing in fast."

"What's happening?" Angus and Glen barged through the kitchen door with Roy on their heels.

"Have any of you fired a gun before?" The commander questioned the group of men around the table; urgency lacing his voice.

"Licensed and trained," Sam said first. Although I'm at a bit of a deficit with my broken wrist, but I'll find a way around it.

"Can't say I have," Angus admitted sheepishly.

"Me neither," Glen followed.

"We've had a couple of lessons at the shooting range yes," Ethan answered for both him and Roy.

"Van, I think your answer is evident. I'm not even going to ask how you got your hands on this much ammunition."

Van shrugged his shoulders without answering.

"Right, listen up. The weapons are all loaded and ready to shoot. Take your pick, and take up positions by the windows and doors. Stay out of sight and wait for my order. Do not shoot and do not come out of hiding until I say so! Got it?"

The men did as the commander instructed and hastily took up their positions behind the window dressings, inside cupboards and behind the couches. On the wooden porch outside the house the shuffling of feet alerted them to the fact that their attackers were on the doorstep and about to access the house. The commander silently signaled to his soldiers, one of whom stuck a tiny optic cable through a hole between the wooden planks at one of the windows. He signaled back that he had eyes on four hostiles. Ready and with their fingers on the triggers, the group of men anticipated the impending attack on the house. Sam's left hand was clammy against the handle of his gun as the barrel rested on his broken wrist. He secretly prayed it provided sufficient stability and that his aim wouldn't be off by too much. Glen and Angus hid behind the drapery on either side of a window; their faces ashen with fear.

The handle on the front door turned slowly, sending ripples of fear through the charged atmosphere in the house. More feet scuffled on the porch outside and Glen jumped when the latch on the window next to him rattled. It became evident that they were completely surrounded and outnumbered by the approaching assailants. Van fought the urge to blast his gun off through the door from behind the couch. Anger overwhelmed his usually composed demeanor. As if he could read his mind the commander shook his head at Van and held up his hand for him to be patient and wait. The front door rattled against another attempt by the attackers to open it. It was locked. Moments later an axe sliced through the wood of the front door, followed by several more strikes. Two hostiles barged through the door. They were entirely oblivious to the fact that the house was occupied by the commander and his army of men. From where they stood they could not see any of the soldiers or the relief members hiding out.

The two hostile men stood in the middle of the foyer and took in the quiet dark surroundings of the farm house. Satisfied it seemed unoccupied the leader finally spoke in his native language and one by one his men entered the house through the front door behind them. Their postures relaxed as they moved through the house and eventually reported back to their leader that there was no one inside the house except them. Loud cheers echoed through the house as they foolishly celebrated their luck.

And when they least expected it, Commander Burger signaled his men to deploy from their places of hiding. The soldiers opened fire at the posse of eighteen surprised men who had assembled in the middle of the kitchen.

In a matter of minutes the frenzied shootout subsided and dead bodies covered the kitchen floor.

"Clear!" one of the soldiers reported followed by two more reports that the enemy had been taken down.

"I need a Scotch," Angus said as he flopped down on the couch in the sitting room.

"You might need to change your pants first, mate," Glen said behind his hand nodding his head towards the dark patch across Angus' groin area.

"Ah bugger," the Scotsman replied embarrassed.

"Happens to the toughest of men, Angus. All in a day's work," Sam replied in an attempt to brush it away.

Angus disappeared down the passage to the bedroom.

When Elaine emerged from the bunker and lay eyes on the bloodbath in her self-claimed kitchen, she shrieked and buried her head in Glen's shoulder.

"There, there my dear, it's all over now. Why don't you take a seat in the sitting room instead? We'll clean up this mess." Glen ushered her toward the lounge before turning back to the kitchen.

Elaine's piercing screams followed by a muffled moan filled the house. The commander charged to where he met two armed black men in the lounge. They had their arms around Angus and Elaine's necks from behind and their guns pointed at their heads.

Shielded by Angus and Elaine's tensed bodies, the two black men shouted panicked orders in their language at the commander. The commander had his gun pointed back at them; his arm sturdy in front of his face.

The one man shouted at him again, this time pushing the barrel of his gun hard against Elaine's temple. She flinched and then broke out into an anguished sob. It angered the man and he pulled his arm tighter around her neck. Her body quaked with terror. The man shouted at the commander again. This time the army leader responded.

"English; speak English!"

The attacker spat onto the floor in front of Elaine causing her face to twist into a grimace to one side. The man scowled and muttered obscenities at the commander before pushing his gun hard against Elaine's cheek.

"Let them go," the commander chanced.

Three soldiers sneaked in behind the two hostage keepers who were unaware of their presence. It was only when they spotted the red laser beams on the floor in front of them that the one who held Elaine captive caught on.

"You can't win here, let them go," the commander warned again.

The man's nostrils flared as he nervously looked back to see the commander's men standing firm in a shooting stance behind them. He was trapped and outnumbered, and even if he shot and killed both Elaine and Angus, it meant the end for them too. The sobering thought didn't stop him. Instead, it angered him further and he mumbled something to his partner under his breath. The two men instantly reacted by turning their backs to each other, all the while holding Angus and Elaine firmly in a tight grip in front of each of them. If the soldiers shot from either angle now they would certainly also kill Angus and Elaine and possibly each other.

The soldiers were not prepared for the clever maneuver on their enemies' part and remained in position. Back to back the two attackers shuffled their hostages toward the front door.

Helpless the commander watched them drag Angus and Elaine out onto the porch. Contrary to Elaine's panicked sobs, Angus clung in submissive silence to his assailant's arm that choked him across his chest. With his men next to him in the house, there was nothing the commander could do at this point apart from allowing it to play out.

When the hostage keepers shuffled their way out onto the porch and down the steps, still with their hostages shielding their bodies, a single gunshot exploded through the air. Elaine fell to her knees and before anyone could react, a second shot was fired and Angus fell to the ground.

The commander and his men charged forward to where Van stood over the two dead kidnappers' bodies; smoking gun in hand.

Elaine didn't move until she felt the warm thick liquid run down the side of her face and a drop of blood splattered onto the dirt in front of her. She screamed the most anguished scream imaginable; fully under the impression she had been shot. It was only when the soldiers helped her and Angus to their feet that she noticed the blood drenched bodies behind her and she realized the blood wasn't hers. A moment later she fainted.

Van held two fingers over his brow as he saluted the commander. He wasn't mocking him. Instead, he was thanking him; grateful that he had the opportunity to take revenge while simultaneously pleading his patriotism to a country he loved so much. Killing wasn't something he was proud of even though he had saved the lives of two innocent people. But he was faced with unsurmountable odds that left him with no other option.

"The first time is always the hardest," the commander spoke as he saluted Van back. "You'll never get over it but you can stand proud that you fought for what was right. If you hadn't intervened both Angus and Elaine would have been dead. That much I can tell you for certain. You saved them, Van. What you did was extremely brave."

Van nodded and rubbed the sweat from his bald head. "I hope I never have to do this again, my friend."

And with that the two men disappeared into the safety of the farmhouse.

CHAPTER SEVENTEEN

ICCRU HEADQUARTERS - LONDON

Matt Fletcher paced the length of his office. It had been several days since they lost contact with Alex and the team and knowing Volkov was after the tooth had him uneasy.

"I have the general on line two for you Matt. It's urgent." His assistant announced over the intercom. Matt rushed to his desk and eagerly lifted the receiver to his ear.

"General, please tell me you have a lead?"

"Affirmative Matt, we found the plane. It crashed just north of the airport. They never landed."

Matt bit down on his jaw and rubbed the back of his neck. "Any fatalities?"

"It appears they might have evacuated prior to the crash. The wreckage is scattered in a field. They're still searching for any survivors but so far my men haven't located any bodies. We found the crate containing the parachutes empty, so we suspect they might have jumped before the plane went down."

"Great work, General. Send me the details of the rendezvous point. I'm on my way."

It was shortly before sunrise the next day when Matt's parachute touched ground in the Kalahari desert just outside the Namibian border. Upon the general's advice it was the safest place to enter South Africa. He had a few miles on foot to his pick-up point. The red rippled Kalahari sand gave way under his feet making it particularly strenuous to walk in and even without the sun up yet it was hot; the steady breeze drying the sweat on his brow almost instantly. He fixed his eyes on the horizon and checked his GPS coordinates. According to his map the desert would subside about three miles south where he should find the dirt road and another mile down that road toward the East the ground team should be waiting for him.

A puff adder slithered across the mesmerizing sand about five yards ahead of him and the sudden surprise caused him to jolt. The desert might look arid and serene, but it was very much alive. He needed to stay alert. In the distance he heard what he suspected were hyenas. There was no way of knowing how far away they were but he wasn't about to take any chances. He kept moving — as fast as it was possible to walk in the thick sand.

The deep orange line that threatened across the horizon signaled the sunrise was imminent. It was a spectacular sight that brought about a sense of relief knowing he wouldn't feel as exposed to early morning predators. He stopped briefly for a drink of water at the foot of a large sand dune. It would be his seventh dune to climb since he landed with his parachute and his unpracticed legs were feeling the strain. Navigating through the red sand was relentless so he paused a bit longer than he had intended and heard movement in the sand behind him. He froze. Without turning around, his mind raced through a list of possible dangers. Nomads were prominent, so were the tribal bushmen. Neither posed a threat to him so he dismissed these. He recalled the hyenas and ruled that it was most likely them. Keeping his body still he slowly turned his head sideways and squinted his eyes to one corner to try catch a glimpse of what was behind him. If it were the hyenas or worse, lions, he'd be trapped between them and the high dune in front of him — and outrun them he couldn't. He swallowed hard turning his head even further to the right. He saw nothing. Confused he decided to look to his left just to be safe so he repeated the exercise over his left shoulder. He still saw nothing. Deciding it was time to slowly attempt turning his torso around, he did and much to his relief, spotted a small group of wild meerkats that curiously sat erect on their hind legs. Matt exhaled and turned to fully face them. This mess with Volkov had him on edge.

"You gave me the fright of my life you little critters. If you're looking for food, I'm out. But I can do with the company climbing this dune."

The meerkats scattered as soon as Matt spoke. Somewhat disappointed he started up the hill alone; laughing at himself for entering into a conversation with the meerkats. His fears were short-lived once he reached the dune ridge and caught sight of the dirt road below. A quick look through his binoculars confirmed the ground team was already waiting for him at the pick up point.

A few hours later he stood in the field assessing the plane wreckage.

"Glad you could join us, Sir."

"What do you have for me Lieutenant?"

"We're trying to make sense of things. So far we found both pilots dead in the cockpit. Strange thing is, they weren't in their seats."

"Someone else was flying the plane?"

"It appears so. There's more. The steering wheel was tied in place by one of the seat belts."

Matt scratched his chin as the lieutenant took him around to the broken off cockpit.

"And the two pilots? What was their cause of death?"

"Both had multiple gunshot wounds to the head and chest. Preliminary forensics suggest the bullets penetrated the cockpit from the outside. They were dead before the plane crashed."

"So that confirms the reason for their initial distress signal. They were already under attack."

"Affirmative, Sir. We also managed to locate three of the four engines so far and recovered several bullets in all of them. They might have flown on only one engine. With nowhere to land it seemed impossible to stay in the air for very long. There's also no further indication that there were any more fatalities at this stage, Sir. My men combed the area over half a mile yesterday and found nothing. Trackers have been at it since 4 a.m. this morning expanding the search to a mile."

"Good job Lieutenant, let me know if your men find something."

Matt hunched at the pile of personal effects next to the wreckage. He picked up the reporter's camera. There's not a chance any reporter would ever part with his camera unless there was absolutely no other option. He checked for the SD card. It was gone. Ok, so he was sharp enough to remove it. The nearby laptop was badly charred. He doubted they'd be able to recover anything from that.

"Sir, my men found something." The lieutenant interrupted a short while later and beckoned for Matt to follow him on foot. "We found several deployed parachutes just outside the half mile point east from here. It's ours. There are fatalities."

A short walk later the two men hovered over the two dead bodies at their feet. Matt felt his chest tighten as they approached Geoffrey and Murray's bodies still tangled under their parachutes in the field.

"Gunshot wounds. Most likely before they even touched ground," the lieutenant commented. One was a relief member from Scotland and the other, a soldier from the South African Defense Force.

Matt placed his hands on his hips and looked across the field. It wasn't quite light already and the sun's first rays cast silhouettes against its orange background.

"What is this place?" Matt asked turning ninety degrees.

"I believe we're on a private cattle farm, Sir."

"Is that a house?" Matt pointed out in front of him, squinting against the sun rising behind the farm house.

"Get down!" The lieutenant promptly ordered in light of this new discovery. He instructed his men to move in and investigate further. His team moved stealthily through the tall grass ducking down every few seconds. As they approached the house, the porch light flashed on and off several times.

"I think it's morse code," Matt declared to the lieutenant as he watched through his binoculars. "I'm a bit rusty. Can you read it?"

The lieutenant fine-tuned the lens of his binoculars. "Looks like it spells *allies*." He radioed his men to respond with SADF and a minute later the porch light followed suit.

"It's them!" The lieutenant exclaimed and pushed the button on his radio. "Move in with caution. I repeat. Proceed."

"Roger that Lieutenant."

The squad moved toward the house and moments later the front door opened and Commander Burger stepped out onto the porch.

. . .

"Commander Burger, 2nd Paratrooper Regiment Pretoria," saluting the lieutenant who promptly saluted back announcing his rank.

"Lieutenant Botha, 24th Infantry Winfield. What's your status, Sir?"

"Unit is secure. A few casualties but all is under control. We lost comms with HQ and three of our men are in the field."

"Matt Fletcher, ICCRU HQ. Where's Hunt?" Matt barged in pushing past the two service men.

"Deployed in the field, Sir. She decided not to abort her mission. Dr. Quinn is inside."

Matt followed the lieutenant through to the kitchen where the remaining relief crew and Sam waited for the all clear.

"You're Sam Quinn I presume?" Matt, equal in height to Sam, bombastically approached him.

"Well, if you're going to be that abrupt about it, I guess I'm forced to own up? Who's asking?" Sam replied cheekily.

"Matt Fletcher, ICCRU. Where's Alex?"

"She's on the mission you recruited her for, remember? Somewhere out there chasing your tooth."

Matt bit down on his jaw. "Can I have a private word with you please Dr. Quinn?"

"Sure, but only if you drop the title."

Matt wasn't smiling at Sam's humor and stormed out into the sitting room.

"You were supposed to accompany her, Dr. Quinn. Why are you here? Who is she with?"

Sam lifted his splinted wrist. "I don't think I had much of a choice now, did I? My injury could have jeopardized our safety. We thought it best she go at it without me. She has two of Burger's men with her."

"And Volkov?" Matt asked with apprehension.

"Volkov? What the hell are you talking about? You mean the Russian billionaire who just built the Mars shuttle? What does he have to do with this?"

Matt turned away and scratched the back of his head. He didn't answer.

"Dammit Fletcher, are you telling me Volkov is somehow involved with this?"

Matt nodded and took a seat on the couch; resting his elbows on his knees.

"We have Intel he's after the tooth, yes. Why, we haven't figured out yet, but I know this man — all too well and my gut tells me it's not to demystify history. He's up to something. He's far too conceited to do this in secret."

Sam watched as Matt's knuckles grew white under his clenched hands. There was certainly history between these two men; and whatever it was showed. Matt got up and walked to the window.

"How long has she been gone? Has she made contact at all?"

"She left a couple of days ago. We have no way of getting in touch with her. Our Sat phone took a bullet and they've been trying to somehow establish contact with HQ since."

Sam's tone changed to anger. "You know she's out there totally exposed. You promised her she'd be protected. Who knows if she's even still alive?"

Matt placed his hands on his hips. "Did she say where she was headed?"

"Professor Graham's office at the Wits University."

"Great!"Matt swung around and stormed out the front door.

"You're welcome!" Sam yelled sarcastically after him as he watched Matt join the lieutenant outside. Knowing there was someone else after the tooth and that Alex was totally unaware of the danger had him break out in a cold sweat. Yes, he had a broken wrist, but his legs still worked, and he knew her thought process. There's no way he'd let her stay out there all by herself. Sam leaped across the lounge and at the door to join the lieutenant and Matt where they studied a map.

"I'm going with you," Sam announced.

"Like hell you are Quinn. You're injured and you could cause more harm than good to this rescue," Matt replied.

"Rescue? Ha, you have another thing coming if you think you're off to rescue Alex. She's tougher than you think Fletcher. I'm quite certain she's several steps ahead of Volkov; or anyone else for that matter. But nonetheless, she's exposed and I know her like the back of my hand. I'm coming with you, and that's final."

Matt folded the map back in his backpack without saying a word.

"Fine, have it your way," he said swinging the pack onto his back. "Lieutenant, I need you to get the others back to the UK safely. Quinn and I will go on to find Hunt. I'll need one of your vehicles and a helicopter on standby at my original pick-up point in the desert. It should be safe and out of sight there until we find a way to reach it."

"Copy that, Sir." The lieutenant agreed and spun on his heels to execute his orders.

"We leave in an hour, Quinn. I'll meet you out back."

An hour later Sam was ready and stood waiting for Fletcher at the barn behind the house. The last bit of the sun's rays hit the roof of the farmhouse where the team was also due to leave shortly. Sam stared across the farmland moments before he felt the thudding pain against the back of his head and fell to the ground.

CHAPTER EIGHTEEN

BACK AT THE ZOO

"There's no way I'm going inside that cage Alex! Forget it."

Alex giggled while holding the blank pages of the leather book out in front of her; hinting for Ezra to use his lighter again. He did, anxiously keeping his eye on the vicious gorilla who paced the inside of its cage behind them.

"X marks the spot and this is definitely it." Alex slammed the book closed and stuck it back down her shirt. Searching the cage with her eyes she recited the clue over and over.

> *Between jackets and spines lie the hidden root that reveals to all the submerged foot.*

"Hidden root, hidden root," Alex chimed. "Root of a tree, root of a problem maybe, rooted in something, rooting for someone."

Alex walked up and down along the fence while the male

primate followed her every step along the inside of the fence; grunting angrily. Her eyes searched every inch of the cage for anything that lined up with the clue, but nothing did. Something just wasn't adding up. Hand on hip she let out a deep sigh and turned away from the cage.

"It's got to be here somewhere. This is the exact spot Professor Graham marked in the book."

She faced the starving silverback again, staring into his black eyes.

"Speak to me gorilla. Where did the professor hide the clue?"

The gorilla studied her pensive face. His black angry eyes relaxed and he stared back at her with deep and desperate sadness that touched the very depths of her heart. Behind him his weak female sat with their baby clinging on for dear life. Still nowhere closer to an answer Alex flipped the lid off the metal trunk she had pulled out of the storage behind the enclosure and tossed several pieces of nearly rotten fruit and vegetables over the fence. There was no way of saving these animals right now. She'd have to hope the zookeepers somehow managed to get them to safety but the food would at least sustain them a little while longer.

The male gorilla scooped several pieces of fruit up and delivered it into his female's lap before going back for more. Alex could have sworn his tender eyes communicated his gratitude. As enormous as they were, in that moment, they seemed very human to her and she continued throwing fruit over the fence. Midway through catapulting the last watermelon into the pen she suddenly stopped.

"It's a bloody red herring! Of course! How did I not see it? Light it again, Ezra!" Alex yelled; excitement exploding from her voice as she flipped open the book's pages and stuffed it under Ezra's nose.

Ezra who had anxiously been watching the gorilla's every move jerked at her sudden command and flicked the cap of his lighter open.

"It was right here all along."

"What was?" Ezra fumbled with his lighter once again holding it under the book's empty pages.

"Lower, more, more, there! See it?"

Ezra cocked his head sideways. "Ok, it's a string of numbers. The combination to the lock on the gorilla's cage?"

Alex knelt down in the patch of dirt next to the cage and enthusiastically copied the numbers into the sand.

"No, it's not actually in the gorilla's cage. It's not even anywhere at the zoo."

"What are you talking about? The map brought us here. X marked the spot."

"Yes, that's what he wanted us to think. He intentionally led us astray; threw us off the trail."

Ezra stared at her with a blank expression on his face.

"Look it's very simple. The clue said the hidden root lay between jackets and spines. The root is R-O-O-T as in solution, not the root of a tree. The root is the actual solution which he hid in this book. Except it wasn't the map. That was a decoy. It was the submerged foot."

"Yeah you're still not making any sense, Alex. I wasn't the brightest at school but as far as I know submerge means to put something under water and well, a foot is a foot."

"That's what's so genius. The professor wanted us to think literally about the clues, but deciphering cryptic is often parables or abstract. The word 'submerge' can also mean to conceal or be hidden and the word 'foot' in this case is the foot of the page. So the hidden solution was at the foot of the page. See? It's the numbers."

Ezra scratched his head but slowly lit up as he pieced it all together. He watched Alex fervently scratch in the dirt.

"So what do we do with all these numbers? What does it even mean?"

"Simple, it's an alphabet replacement clue. Look, each number represents a letter of the alphabet. A = 1, B = 2, and so on, and these numbers, my dear friend, spell out RISING STAR."

Ezra shook his head and laughed. "Who are you again? I have no idea how you know all this but I've never seen anything like it. You are like an amplified Lara Croft."

He turned to face the gorillas devour their small supply of food.

"What do you think will happen to them?"

"I'm not sure, Ezra, but as much as I'd like to help them, we have to get out of here. Volkov is a smart man. I have no doubt he'll catch up to us very soon. It's getting dark. If we can get a head start right now and get out of the city tonight it might just be our saving grace."

Alex got up and kicked dirt over the numbers to bury the clue.

"Any idea what this clue means?" Ezra asked as he tossed the last medley of vegetables over the enclosure's fence.

"You bet. The professor's hidden the tooth back in the very place the rest of the bones were found — The Rising Star."

"Great, and that is what exactly?"

"It's the very cave Homo *naledi* was excavated. It's at the Cradle of Humankind. Let's go."

Outside the zoo they arrived to where their car had been ransacked entirely. The wheels had been stolen and the steering wheel was missing.

"Oh come on!" Ezra shouted. "It's those bloody kids. Now what?"

"We walk until we find another one. Let's go. Be alert."

Walking the empty streets of Johannesburg at night was suicide, even in normal circumstances. Doing it in the middle of a civil outbreak was ludicrous, but they had no other option. With their rifles on their hips, they set off down the road in search of another vehicle. The sun had just about fully set and it was as if the ghost town during the day had suddenly come alive with gangs and violent criminals who used the obscurity of the night to their full advantage. As they were about to turn the corner at the end of the block Ezra, who was walking in front, stopped and pulled Alex back against the wall. An army tanker was working its way down the quiet street towards them. If they were seen they'd be detained indefinitely. They ran in the opposite direction and hid in a narrow alley behind rotten food delivery cardboard boxes. A few rats scattered noisily under their feet causing Alex's heart to skip several beats. When the tanker had passed and there was enough distance between them, they slipped out from behind the garbage and ran up another side road. From a block of flats above their heads screams echoed through the darkness followed by a crying baby. Alex forced herself not to think about the possible causes thereof and pushed on with caution. A few blocks further a small supermarket's lights illuminated the dark sidewalk in front of them.

"Think we can stop to get something to eat and drink?" Ezra asked. "We're likely not going to find another one open."

"I don't know Ezra. He shouldn't even be open at this time of night under these circumstances. Let's keep going."

"Not sure I can Alex. I'm starving. We'll be in and out, ok?"

"Sure, but let's make it quick," Alex reluctantly gave in and they proceeded into the store.

A man of Indian descent apprehensively went for his gun under the counter as soon as he saw them in their combat attire, scaring his tabby cat off the counter and into hiding under one of the shelves.

"It's cool my friend, we're Defense Force," Ezra calmed the

man. "We're on patrol just looking for something to eat, all's good."

The man nodded and directed them to the back of the shop where he had a small supply of fresh sandwiches.

"One would think he'd be hiding in his home," Alex whispered to Ezra as they headed toward the back of the shop.

"I guess he's desperate to put food on the table. Tuna or Ham?"

"I'm not much of a fish person," Alex replied back as she took the Ham and Cheese sandwich from his hand. Ezra turned and scooped two Coca Colas from the fridge. Above their heads, in the overhead mirror, Alex caught a glimpse of two hooded men walking into the shop and a second later they heard the shopkeeper beg for his life. Obscured by the tall shelving, Alex pulled Ezra down behind the shelf and out of the mirror's reflection as she instantly concluded the store was being robbed. Her heart pounded loudly in her ears as she listened to them threaten the Indian shop owner. They weren't out to save the world tonight, but there they were; caught in the middle of calamity and conscience. While one of the thugs instructed the shopkeeper to empty his till and hand over his money, the other skimmed the shop to see if they were alone. Alex and Ezra shuffled quietly between the shelves to remain out of sight. The owner of the shop hesitated to hand over his earnings. The criminal shoved his gun toward the owner and shouted impatiently, slamming his hand loudly onto the counter in front of him. The sudden loud noise frightened the owner's cat out from under the shelf next to Ezra's feet, drawing attention to the back of the shop. Alex lay flat on the floor behind one of the shelves, keeping her eyes on their feet from beneath the shelving. She anxiously watched as one of the burglars made his way toward where Ezra sat huddled behind another shelf. Quick on her feet she took a tin of baked beans off the shelf next to her and rolled it into the opposite direction. The thug stopped inches away from Ezra and swung around quickly at the unexpected noise behind him. Now sensitive to the possibility that someone else was in the shop and that they might not be alone, they instructed the shopkeeper to move out from behind his counter and down the aisle passing to the right of Ezra's shelf. He did so grudgingly; pushed forward by the thug's gun in his ribs. On the left side of the shelf the second thug walked down, gun pointed out in front of his nose. From where Alex hid two shelves away she watched as they moved closer to where Ezra still sat hidden at the foot of the shelf with nowhere to go.

Her mind searched frantically for the best way out and, automatically found her body moving back up the aisle towards the front of the shop. She'd surprise them from behind and hopefully, create enough distraction for Ezra and the shop owner to get away from them for long enough for her to help them escape somehow. Alex pushed a container of loose candy off the counter onto the floor. The thugs both swung around and fired their guns in her direction. Ezra jumped them from behind, pulling the shopkeeper down onto the floor behind him. Alex dove behind the counter taking cover from the incoming rain of bullets and heard several bullets exchanging at the back of the shop. Above her head the round mirror in the corner of the shop played out a grueling scene between Ezra and both burglars who now opened full gunfire at him. With Ezra's body only half protected by the shelf, he narrowly missed several bullets. What felt like minutes later Alex watched as Ezra shot and killed one of them. Now one man down, the thief was outnumbered and Alex decided to have another go at the remaining gunman. She bobbed up from behind the counter and fired three bullets into his back. He dropped dead to the floor.

With both criminals now dead, Alex rose fully from behind the counter.

"Clear!" she shouted waiting for Ezra to respond. He didn't. Her stomach tightened as she rushed down the aisle to the back of the shop where she found the shop owner sitting on the floor next to Ezra's semi-conscious body.

"No, no, no! Get help!" she shouted at the shopkeeper as she pulled Ezra's barely conscious body across her lap. The shop owner disappeared through a hidden door behind one of the fridges at the back.

"Ezra, stay with me. You're not dying like this, you hear me? Stay with me."

But Ezra couldn't speak. His eyes had dulled over and his breathing slowed down to a shallow pant. Just above the neck of his combat vest a bullet had penetrated his body. Alex tightened his vest in an effort to compress the blood flow.

"Help is coming, ok. Just stay with me."

Behind them the shopkeeper came rushing back into the shop with two burly Indian men at his side. It took just a brief instant for them to lift Ezra up and Alex found herself following them through the secret door, up a dark, narrow flight of stairs into a small apartment on top of the shop.

"No! We need to get him to the hospital," Alex yelled in a panic as they lay him down on a couch.

"He'll bleed to death if we don't get him to a doctor!"

"I have doctor. This Patel, my third cousin, he doctor." The shop owner explained in a thick Indian accent as he hurriedly pushed her out of the way and ushered one of the burly men through.

"He needs a hospital!" Alex tried again but they ignored her.

A short elderly woman, dressed in an olive green sari, pulled her out of the way and to the side of the room. Alex fought off the intense aching pain that gripped her chest as she helplessly watched Patel work on Ezra. Deep regret ripped through her numb body. She should have never agreed to stopping for the stupid sandwich. None of this would have happened. The sequence of events repeated in her mind as she took a sip of the strange herbal tea the woman gave her and, much to her surprise, observed Patel's medically experienced hands nimbly at work on Ezra's bullet wound. Time seemed to stand still as she waited for a miracle but in the early hours that morning, Ezra T-bone Theron joined his parents in the afterlife.

When Alex finally wiped her tears and lifted her head off Ezra's lifeless body, she slipped her hand inside his pocket and pulled out his father's gold lighter. Her thumb rubbed over the inscription that read *to the bravest man I've ever known.*

The lighter was meant to bring him good luck and look where it got him. But brave he certainly was. Earlier that week this young soldier had not only saved her from Volkov, but also Sam from falling to his death and now the Indian shop keeper from being killed too. He was indeed the bravest man that lived and in her eyes, a true hero.

CHAPTER NINETEEN

Alex rubbed her swollen eyes and temples to relieve the throbbing pain in her head. She looked around the poorly lit tiny apartment and found herself still sitting in the recliner she fell asleep in the night before. She stared at the empty couch where Ezra took his last breath. A pool of dry blood stared back at her. She sat up and skimmed the room around her and found the old lady seated at the tiny round dining table behind her.

"Where's Ezra? What have you done with him?" she yelled out angrily.

The little Indian woman didn't answer. Alex threw the quilt off her legs and walked over to her.

"Where's my friend? Where's your son?"

Still the old woman didn't answer her. Instead she pointed her henna painted hand toward the stairs. Alex swung around and made her way down the dirty, narrow stairwell to the secret entrance into the fateful shop below where she found the shop owner scrubbing the pools of blood off the floor. The sight horrified Alex and she fought back the urge to run past him and out the front door.

The shop keeper jumped to his feet and ushered her away from the spot where Ezra was shot.

"What have you done with him? Where is my friend?" Alex asked with fresh tears streaming down her face.

"Patel he take good care of your friend. I'm too sorry for your friend. Come, sit, sit." The shopkeeper's English was poor but his condolences punched a hollow hole through her stomach as she sat down on the stool behind the shop counter. Alex found herself looking up into the overhead mirror where she watched the shooting play out the night before. Regret filled her once again and she buried her face in her hands.

"Calm, calm lady, please? Your friend he save my life. You save my life. I die yesterday but no, you save me. What you want huh? I give you all I got. Here, take for you."

The Indian shop owner pulled a few hundred rand notes from his hidden drawer under his till and stuffed it in her numb hands. She pushed it away.

"I don't need your money."

"What I give you want, huh? Say, I give you anything."

Alex wiped her face and looked up at the small Indian man whose desperate brown eyes pleaded for her forgiveness and a chance to repay her. It wasn't his fault either, she thought. It was just an unforeseen event that neither of them could have prevented. He too will be scarred by this for the rest of his life.

"Do you have a car?" She asked softly, blowing her nose on a tissue he handed her.

"You want car? No problem lady, my pleasure!" The shop owner ran upstairs and a minute later appeared with a single silver key hanging from a gold and black plushy die.

"You keep, no problem."

Alex took the key from his eager hand; his burdened eyes now filled with joy.

"Thank you for your help. I'm sorry too," she whispered and allowed him to drag her by the arm through the backdoor of the shop past the apartment staircase into an adjacent gated alley where his car was parked.

W hen Alex settled into the rusty gold Honda that matched the die dangling from its key, she felt lost for the first time in a very long time. She missed Sam's strength and found herself wondering what he would've said to lift her spirits right now. She had no means of communicating with him on the farm and she shot up a prayer for his safety. Hopefully by some miracle they had managed to repair their communications pack and had called for help.

In front of her the streets outside the city lay quiet. Evidence of vandalism from the night before stuck out its ugly head every now and again but for the most part, it was relatively peaceful. Her mind wandered to Volkov and if perhaps he might have caught on to her. She had lost a lot of time and he could already be hot on her trail by now. Her eyes scanned the rearview mirror every couple of minutes but thankfully, there was no one in sight for miles and she was relieved to have an opportunity to reflect on her own thoughts.

But, when Alex approached the tiny rural settlement en route to The Cradle of Humankind, she slowed the car down. Up ahead, the road was closed off by thick wooden poles positioned in a crossbar across the road. The horizontal pole was draped in wired fencing and large fires stood on either side. Armed men with bandanas covering their mouths, stood guard on both ends. She stopped a quarter of a mile away and took a closeup view through her binoculars. Her eye caught Ezra's backpack on the passenger seat that the shopkeeper threw into the car last minute. Her insides felt heavy as she realized she couldn't take the men on alone. She forced her mind back to the dire situation at hand and turned to look at the road behind her. There was no way around the barricade and the guards looked to be more hostile than friendly. She looked down at the map in her lap. The only way to the Cradle would be through them or through the field to her right, and she wasn't sure this Honda would make it. As she contemplated her next move, her eyes went up to her rearview mirror and saw a black jeep fast approaching her from behind. She flung her head around and realized it was Volkov.

Unladylike words escaped from under her clenched jaw. She had no idea how he had managed to find her without deciphering the zoo's decoy. Her heart raced under the pressure of finding a way to bypass the barricade in front of her while simultaneously escaping Volkov behind her. She shifted the gear lever into first gear and tightened her hands around the steering wheel. The Honda puffed a big cloud of smoke from the exhaust as she revved the accelerator. It was now or never, she thought and without another second to spare she pushed her foot flat onto the pedal and screeched the wheels of her gold chariot toward the barred road ahead. Much to her surprise the Honda performed under the pressure and bolted down the tarmac. Straight ahead the armed guards jumped into position and flung their rifles off their shoulders and in front of them. A succession of shots fired from their weapons rained down onto the Honda's bonnet and through her front window. Alex hunched down into her seat and kept going. Behind her Volkov's men fired back, but much to her surprise, not at her but the guards. A few yards away from the cross pole Alex pulled her hand brake up and yanked the steering wheel to the right. The car slid sideways across the road before veering off into the rough on the side of the road. She shifted gears and forced the steering wheel back to the left, pushing her foot flat onto the accelerator. Vaguely conscious of one of the guards being shot dead to her left by one of Volkov's men, she forced the car into a forward direction and pushed the noisy Honda through the rough and around the barricade. The wheels hit several large rocks that sent Alex off her seat but she kept going; several times almost losing control of the car. Dirt clouds behind her car made it impossible to see through the rearview mirror what was unfolding behind her, but there was no stopping now. She had to keep going forward — for as long and far as the rust bucket would take her.

With her heart threatening to push through her chest and combat vest, and her legs feeling like jelly, she sped down the road through the rural settlement. A stray dog unexpectedly ran across the road forcing Alex to swerve hard to avoid it. Unable to maneuver the car back onto the road, she hit a makeshift street vendor's tin shack, sending him diving out into the bushes to avoid being killed. Several bags of oranges hit her front window blocking her vision, so she pulled the steering wheel to the right in the direction of the road she was on prior to the incident. Two of the Honda's wheels lifted off the ground as she fought to maintain control of the car again. Her hands ached under the strain of the steering wheel when all four wheels gripped the tarmac underneath her again. Somehow she managed to gain control of the car and found herself racing down the road. Frantic villagers scattered into all directions away from the road as the gold car sped past them. Adrenaline pushed through her veins and Alex looked back in her rearview mirror for the first time again. Behind her a truck with five or six angry hooligans on the back raced toward her. Volkov was nowhere to be seen. Her eyes repeatedly searched both sideview mirrors but the black Jeep was nowhere in sight. In that moment she wasn't sure if she was relieved or worried that she'd now face having to fight the truck full of angry men behind her on her own again. She pushed on down the empty road away from the settlement and knew the road to the Cradle of Humankind heritage site wasn't far down the road. She'd have to shake them off first though. Her hand went to Ezra's backpack next to her and she stuck her hand into the front pocket. Unable to take her eyes off the road her hands identified the oblong shape of a hand grenade. Her strained mouth curled into a soft smile as she silently thanked him for his secret weaponry.

A sudden boulder in the middle of the road caught her off guard and she swerved out to avoid it just in time. The truck behind her followed suit and was closing in on her. She pushed the Honda harder, but to no avail. Her hand reached for the grenade in Ezra's backpack and she knocked the shattered driver's window to her right out with her elbow. Her teeth gripped the steel pin as she pulled it out and tossed the grenade through the window in the road behind her. Her timing was impeccable as the grenade exploded directly under the nose of the truck sending her assailants through the air. Fear made way for an exhilarated rush of success soaring through her every cell and she wished Ezra or Sam were there to celebrate her escape with her. Somehow she felt they both helped her; Ezra by means of a realm beyond her present one, and Sam through thought transference.

Still there was no sign of Volkov and his team. It was entirely possible they had been killed by the armed guards, but there was no way of knowing for sure. No body, no murder, she thought. She had to assume they were still alive and stay alert.

A few yards further the road to the heritage site came into view and Alex slowed to turn into it. She wriggled upright into her seat and leaned forward onto the steering wheel affording her a clearer view between the bullet holes in the front window. The long winding road leading up to the entrance was completely deserted. On either side of the road dry grass stretched out for miles in all four directions. It was as if she was in the middle of a barren land with nothing around her. In the parking lot an abandoned bus stood to one side and a couple of bicycles were still chained to a tree. Using the bus to conceal her car she parked up but kept her eyes fixed on her surroundings — just in case. Satisfied she was alone, she emptied Ezra's backpack on the seat next to her. Aside from one wrinkled decolorized photo he had no personal effects in the bag. The faded image in the photo caught her eye. It was a young Ezra standing between his multiracial parents. Alex slid three more bullets into his gun's magazine. Her thoughts drifted to her own parents and she wondered if she'd ever see them again. Willing her mind into the present she grabbed spare ammunition and tucked two grenades into her backpack. With his loaded gun in her waistband at the front of her pants and her gun reloaded and ready in her hand, she slowly climbed out of the car.

CHAPTER TWENTY

Nature's silence was deafening as she stood surrounded by fields of dry grassland. A soft warm breeze touched her skin while she cautiously set off down the footpath towards the dome shaped building that was entirely covered in grass. A large sign displayed the name 'Maropeng' and hung above four glass doors that spanned the entrance from left to right —they were all locked. She took a few steps back and looked over her shoulder before firing a bullet through one of them, shattering shards of glass everywhere.

Inside, the exhibition centre was dark and Alex switched on her flashlight. The large hall showcased a multitude of rare fossils marking the evolution of the human race. Aside from her rubber-soled combat boots squeaking on the shiny floor, it was as silent as it was outside. She paused in front of the lifelike upright replica of Homo *naledi* and studied his face under torchlight. If only he knew how much trouble he'd caused, she thought.

She explored the prospect of Professor Graham hiding the tooth inside this reproduction and inspected the glass casing around his hairy human-like body. It was entirely sealed. She second guessed whether she might have misunderstood the alphabet clue. Her mind recalled her writing in the sand at the zoo. She should double check it. She sat cross-legged on the cold floor and pulled the leather book from its hiding place inside her shirt. Her hand reached for Ezra's lighter from within her backpack and she flicked a flame underneath the page. She ran through the code in her head. It clearly spelled out 'Rising Star'. Satisfied she slammed the book closed, tucked it back down her shirt and slipped Ezra's lighter into her pants' pocket instead; it might just rub off some good luck. It was decided then. She needed to find the Rising Star cave.

Back on her feet she shone her torchlight, out in front of her face and turned in a three hundred and sixty degree circle. There was no signage pointing to the cave anywhere. Hastily she worked her way through the massive exhibition hall searching for a map or exhibit that would provide any clues to the cave's exact location, but, apart from a three dimensional display of the intricate cave system, there were none. Her eyes lingered on a cross section of the cave system on the display wall. There was more than one entrance it seemed and from what she could see, it all pointed to the cave being a fair distance away from the exhibition centre. A slight heaviness took hold of her stomach as she studied the narrow pathways and chutes that ventured a hundred feet deep and displayed tunnels that were only eight inches wide. Photos of the actual excavation showed tunnels only accessible by sliding and wriggling one's body through. Her eyes caught the words 'superman crawl' and 'Dragon's Back' and fear trickled down her spine. There was no denying it; she was scared. In the back of her mind she hoped that perhaps, by some miracle, the professor had hidden the tooth somewhere outside the cave instead. Doubt that she could complete this mission filled her mind. She wasn't a caver by any stretch of the imagination and navigating the narrow tunnels to the Dinaledi chamber where Homo *naledi* was excavated was going to take all the wit and nerve she could muster; not to mention she had no equipment whatsoever. She rubbed her hand across her throat in a futile attempt to relieve the tightness that increased by the minute as she skimmed through the small gallery of photos on the wall. The sudden realization that it would be very dark down there dawned on her and she promptly switched her torch off to preserve the battery.

With her flashlight switched off the hall was so dark she could barely see her hands in front of her face. She shut her eyes and centralized her senses to navigate her way through the expansive space; feeling her way along the glass casings and the walls back to the entrance. A sudden noise at the entrance ahead of her stopped her dead in her tracks. She opened her eyes and strained her ears. There it was again. It sounded like glass crushing under feet followed by squeaking shoes on the floor. Her heart skipped several beats. She wasn't alone. It could only mean Volkov and his men had survived the barricade and were very much alive. Panic numbed her legs as she listened to them coming closer towards her. She pushed her back firmer against the concrete wall. The faded outlines of a large exhibit in front of her came into view. Having seen most of the exhibition hall in torchlight she held somewhat of an advantage over them — but only if it remained dark. Her mind conjured a plan. If she could remain hidden in the dark she could evade them by slipping past them along the outer walls and, once they were further along in the hall, escape through the front doors. Careful not to announce her position and have her soles squeak in reply, she continued at a sloth-like pace on her tip toes along the outer wall, pausing every couple of seconds to assess where they were. The numbing sound of a flashlight's switch bounced off the walls; further confirmed by the sudden bright ray that spilled across the floor about five yards in front of her. She pulled back behind a tall graphic display and narrowly missed the flashlight's beam. Her heart beat wildly in her chest as their footsteps drew closer and closer. She drew in a sharp breath and held it when they moved within a yard from her. If she as much as breathed they'd hear her. She squeezed her eyes shut waiting for them to continue past her. Her gun's waffle-print handle etched marks into her flesh from gripping it too tight. Then they stopped; dead in front of her. Alex identified the silhouettes of at least three men. Their sudden pause caused her leg muscles to tighten as she readied herself to run. If they turned forty degrees to the left with their torchlight they'd see her. Beads of sweat broke out on her lip. It seemed like an eternity frozen in silence, but then, as suddenly as they had stopped, they continued on and walked past her. Once they were a fair distance from her she finally exhaled and took a couple of short shallow breaths instead. She tried taking a small sideways step concentrating on putting her foot down slowly. The floors were not very forgiving of noise and the tiniest of squeaks escaped from beneath her rubber soles. Deciding it was too risky she lay flat on her tummy and raised her feet in the air. She'd slide her way out of there instead. Using the wall to guide her she pushed her body along the floor toward the bright light of the entrance door.

Relief washed over her as she finally reached it and jumped to her feet. Bits of shattered glass made a crushing noise under her shoes as she ran through the entrance and down the path. Convinced the glass under her feet had alerted them of her escape, she ran faster. There was no stopping now. She had to run as fast and as far as her legs could carry her. Her feet thumped hard on the concrete path. As predicted, her departure over the broken glass had alarmed them and they announced their pursuit with a succession of bullets on the concrete next to her feet. A split decision had her veer off the path and into the hip-high grassland. Her eyes caught sight of the signage warning against snakes, but she couldn't divert now. She'd take her chances. Another bullet whisked past her head and she ducked in response. The ground under her feet was unstable but she kept running. A brief turn of her head confirmed it was indeed Volkov's men on her tail. She tried to get her bearings and changed direction. She was out of breath but adrenaline propelled her feet forward. Unannounced she hit a narrow foot-path and took it. A small sign with an arrow which pointed to the right came in sight, so she followed it. Where it led she couldn't say, but it offered a way to escape and that was all that counted. She briefly turned around again and slammed down hard onto the ground when her foot hit a small boulder in the middle of the path. Her arms instantly ejected her off the ground and she scrambled to her feet. There was no one behind her and no bullets flying over her head. It worried her not knowing where her attackers were, but she kept going. A fork in the path forced her to choose between a yellow arrow or a red one. An instant choice had her decide on taking the yellow one. The footpath was far more rugged and she struggled to find her footing. Her lungs burned as she pushed herself to run faster where the path offered the opportunity. Careful not to fall again she turned once more to look behind her. There was still no sight of anyone behind her. Relieved she might have either outrun them or possibly even eluded them when she took the yellow trail, Alex slowed her pace just enough to gather control of her breathing. Her legs were heavy and they ached in the wake of her sprint. She needed to stay focussed, she reminded herself. No time to slack off. She'd get that tooth and ride on out of there with her trusty gold wagon. And with newfound vigor, she continued down the path at a gentle jog.

Her legs were tired but she kept running in the opposite direction away from the Maropeng centre. Eventually the path gave way to large clearings and big shady trees with only a few sparse bushes here and there. Her mouth was dry and the sun's relentless rays beat down hard on her skin. She had no idea how far she had run but, by her calculations, it was at least five miles. Since taking the yellow path, Volkov and his men were nowhere to be seen or heard. Her feet threatened to give way causing her to almost fall more than once. She desperately needed to stop and take a break. Deciding it was safe enough, she stopped running. With her hands on her knees she bent over in an attempt to control her rapid breathing. She was nauseous and the stitch pain in her side forced her to pinch down hard on her waist. Her legs went weak beneath her body as she collapsed in the shade of a large tree. Her shaking legs stretched out in front of her while she leaned her head back against the tree trunk to catch her breath.

It wasn't until she tried to stop the world from spinning that she realized she was about to faint and everything went black in front of her eyes.

The faint sound of men arguing in the distance brought Alex back to consciousness as she forced her heavy eyelids open. She reached her hand up to rub her eyes but couldn't. She tried again, this time lucid enough to realize she was tied down to the very tree she had collapsed against. Confused she tried again; this time with both arms. Thick cords ran across her chest and arms and around the tree behind her. In front of her body, her legs stretched out and were bound together at her ankles. She flung her head sideways and determined the men's voices were coming from about ten yards behind her. To the right of them Volkov sat on a chair in the shade of a large tree whilst admiring his nails. Alex wriggled her arms in an attempt to loosen the rope but it didn't budge. She tried again, this time the rope gave way just a tad. With her arms next to her sides it was easier to curl them. If she kept doing bicep curls she might eventually move the rope higher toward her shoulders and then she could slip out from underneath it.

"Even if you untie yourself, Miss Hunt, you're not getting away from me this time." Volkov's thick Russian accent startled her from behind.

She stopped wriggling and looked straight ahead not saying a word.

CHAPTER TWENTY-ONE

"It seems I do have a purpose for you after all, Alex Hunt." Volkov's deep voice spoke again.

Alex tried to speak but her lips were dry and her tongue stuck to her palate. Deciding it wasn't worth the effort, she dropped her head forward onto her chest. The exertion of the past few days took a toll on her exhausted body. She hadn't eaten much in days and sitting in the hot sun all day added to her already dehydrated state. Volkov snapped his fingers and one of his men ran over to Alex with a bottle of fresh water. He held the bottle of lukewarm water against her lips and made her drink.

"Yes, yes, drink up. You're going to need all the strength you can find Alex. If you haven't noticed, my men are a little bit on the big side and I doubt if even one of their feet will fit down that hole."

Piqued by his last comment Alex looked around to see what hole he was referring to. She didn't realize she was that close to the cave's entrance when she fainted.

"Yes, Alex, thanks to you, you brought us right to the very spot we wanted to be, so let's not waste anymore time finding that tooth."

Volkov barked a command in Russian at his men and two of them immediately rushed to Alex's side and lifted her to her feet. Her leg muscles ached and she felt very weak. She asked for more water and they held the bottle to her mouth again. It helped.

"If you think I'm going to help you find that tooth you're wrong, Volkov."

He laughed sadistically. "I don't think you have much choice, Alex."

He beckoned one of his men over who held out a tablet in front of Alex and pressed play. A sudden feeling of tightness expanded across her chest and ripped her heart in two as Alex watched the moving images of a man tied to a chair. His face was covered with a black hood and his naked body was severely battered and tortured. For a moment Alex stopped breathing as her body went numb with disbelief. It was Sam. She turned her face away when a baseball bat was thrust into his abdomen.

"Turn it off!" She yelled.

He did.

Filled with sadness Alex looked into Volkov's dark eyes that continued to mock her and instantly her tightness turned to hatred and anger. Her hands clenched into fists and her eyes turned cold.

"Let Sam go," she said in a raspy monotone voice.

Volkov sat forward in his chair. "So now you'll do it?"

Alex spat on his shiny black shoes in reply but kept her eyes locked with his.

"All right that's enough time wasting. I don't have all day. Put her in the hole," he instructed.

"You're supposed to be this saint, Volkov, but you're nothing but a fraud and a murderer. You won't get away with this."

"Oh but I already have my dear Alex. That tooth is all that's left for me to find. Once you deliver it to me I'm going to change the world. Genetic engineering is the way of the future and who better to lead the way than me, huh? Have you ever considered how creating a colony of new humans will change this world for the better? Think about it, Alex. I'm one tooth away from a one of a kind re-engineered genus that challenges the human body as you know it. My new species will regenerate cells and heal themselves. Their brain capacity will exceed that of human intellect by three hundred percent and they'll have a muscular economy no mortal can ever possess."

Alex listened as a delirious Volkov declared his plans for an engineered race.

"And then what Volkov? How are us mortals supposed to survive with your engineered humans roaming around? We'll die out faster than you can reproduce them. It will destroy everything on this planet."

"Oh, Alex, you're so short-sighted. I'm not a mass murderer.

Sure I enforce a little bit of torture here and there to get what I want, but mass destruction? I'll leave that to the presidents. You can continue your ridiculous politics and Greenpeace marches all you want. Did you forget I just succeeded in getting the first humans to Mars?"

Alex's eyes grew wide.

"You're building a new human race to go live on Mars? That's preposterous!"

Volkov belted a loud laugh that quite possibly traveled all the way back to Johannesburg.

"I'm a genius, but that's taking it too far, Alex. It's a lot simpler than that. I have already built the world's first utopia space ship — my own Millennium Falcon. Now, no more chit chat, we have a tooth to find."

"You are crazy if you think I'm going to go down that hole, Volkov! It's suicide!" Alex shouted as she tried to loosen his sidekick's grip around her arms.

"For you yes, not for me, or do I need to remind you what's really at stake here? So before you die down there, just make sure you get me my tooth first, ok?" He mocked, his voice dripping in sarcasm.

Volkov nodded to one of his men. The six foot five sidekick scooped Alex up under his arm like he was picking up a toddler and carried her toward a nearby gaping hole next to a large tree.

"You can't let me down there, Volkov! I don't have any caving experience and, besides, how do we know it's even down there?"

"Oh it's down there all right. Our dear professor thought he was clever by leading us to the gorilla instead. He was loyal to a fault even when we sliced a blade in his kneecaps. That's why we needed you, Alex. To finish the puzzle for us. So, unless you want the same fate as our professor, I suggest you get down there."

His men loosened the rope around her shoulders and ankles and removed her combat vest before fastening a knot around her waist. The leather book fell to the ground and Volkov threw her a steely look.

"So you had it all along then. And look where that got you. Now get on with it Alex Hunt. I don't have all day."

"If you send me down that hole you'll never have your tooth, Volkov. I might never come out of there alive."

"I'll take my chances Alex. I heard you're the best so I have every reason to believe you'll make it. Besides, that's why we have the rope tied around your waist. And just in the event you're thinking of escaping, you have three hours or Sam dies."

Alex didn't give him the satisfaction of responding. She threw her shoulders back and fastened her hair in a bun. He had Sam and if the tooth was what he wanted, it was a small price to pay for Sam's freedom.

A lex fought back her tears as they lowered her feet-first into the hole. The rope cut through her thin T-shirt into her flesh and she grabbed onto the rope above her head to alleviate the chafing. The deeper they lowered her the darker it became. Her body quaked as the dirt walls closed in on her.

"Volkov, please? Let's do this the right way! I need equipment to do this? How am I supposed to see anything?"

He didn't answer and Alex was lowered deeper down into the pitch-black hole until her feet finally touched the uneven rocky ground.

"Now find me that tooth, Alex Hunt!" Volkov shouted from above.

Alex let out a soft sob as she tried to see through the blackness. The earthy scent of wet soil filled her nostrils. She reached into her pocket for Ezra's lighter and flicked it on. In the soft light she could see two dark tunnels; one in front of her and one to her left. Behind her and to her right she was closed in between dirt walls. She looked up towards the distant hole above her head. She must have been at least fifty feet deep but it was hard to tell through the darkness. She ventured one step forward and stumbled against something. A gentle breeze from one of the tunnels blew out the lighter's flame in her hand. She flicked the lighter on again and looked down at her feet to find her backpack. Her heart leaped for joy as she knelt down and searched for her torch. When her fingers closed over the cold steel casing of her torch she closed her eyes and quietly exhaled.

The rope around her waist pulled tight, tugging her upward. "Hurry up Alex! Time is money!" Volkov shouted from above.

"Come down and get it yourself then!" She shouted back unable to mask her frustration with the predicament she found herself in. Her mind recalled the images of the tight spaces in the tunnels from the diagram in the exhibit. Her stomach rolled and she felt as if she was going to drown in fear. To her annoyance the rope pulled tight again and she swore at them in response. The two tunnels were equally frightening to her and choosing one over the other proved fatal no matter which way she looked at it. Her mind wandered to her poor choice of following the yellow path before. Her torchlight swung from one to the other and finally, she opted to go down the tunnel directly in front of her. She crossed her fingers and hoped it would lead to the tooth.

Alex drew in a deep breath and shone her torch around the entrance to the tunnel. She recalled Volkov saying the professor left clues. Her eyes searched the walls but there was nothing apart from limestone. She was about to take her first step and paused as the thought crossed her mind to look to the floor. Her lips broke into a relaxed smile when, in the faintest glow of her flashlight, a carving appeared on a dolomite rock formation under her foot. She knelt down to have a closer look. It was Roman numerals.

CXXII

"One hundred and twenty-two," she said out loud as she brushed away the dirt around it with her fingers. "One hundred and twenty-two what, Professor?" She spoke in the air and studied the tunnel more closely. It was no more than fifty inches in diameter so taking proper paces would prove difficult. Deciding to wager on it being toe-to-heel paces, she hunched her body forward and navigated her way through the tunnel while counting off the one hundred and twenty-two foot-to toe-paces.

It was hot and difficult to breathe. Her head knocked on the protruding ridges of the limestone and dolomite stones in the cavity walls. The most recent bump had sliced through her skin and blood trickled down the side of her face. Roughly a hundred and twenty-two paces further she paused and inspected the walls. There was nothing. No further evidence of anything buried there. It was impossible to turn around in the tight space so she directed her flashlight down the tunnel in front of her, wondering if it would open up soon. All the while she kept her eyes on the walls for any clues. She concluded the professor's feet were a lot bigger than hers so she add a few more feet. Her assumption paid off when the tunnel forked only a few feet further.

"Great, another fork," she muttered.

Again she scanned the walls of the tunnel entrance and spotted the small, brown marking of an arrow above her head. It clearly pointed to the right tunnel which was even smaller than the one she'd come from and only allowed passage by means of sliding on her tummy. She checked the knot of the guide rope around her waist and secured it in place. The space was tight as she lay down flat. Her shoulders wedged between the sides of the underground passage and it was hard to breath. Stings of pain shot through her elbows as they scraped on the sharp edges of the tunnel floor. She pushed and shoved, wriggling her body sideways in places and willed her mind away from the confined claustrophobic space. And just as she thought she had mastered the tunnel, she hit a stone wall. Again, fear threatened to push her into hysteria but she fought her mind to stay calm. She had crawled a good ten yards. Going in reverse was going to be incredibly challenging. It took everything not to break down in tears and she momentarily dropped her chin onto the coarse dirt and shut her eyes. Her mind recalled the tortured images of Sam who was depending on her to get through this and save him — for once. She lifted her head and sniffed back the tears resolving to dig her heels in and reverse. She lifted her torchlight and froze. In front of her, above the very stone that prevented her from moving forward, she looked at the single stalactite that hung down from the ceiling. Alex frowned. Usually one found stalactites inside a large cave chamber; not like this inside a narrow tunnel. She slithered closer, reached up and pulled it. Dirt fell down onto her head and a creaky noise came from the stone wall in front of her as it loosened from the sides.

When the creaking stopped Alex pushed it forward and the stone rolled out into a massive chamber. Alex felt her chest open up as, for the first time inside the cave system, she was able to breathe easily again as relief washed over her.

The chamber lit up under her torchlight to reveal glistening stalactites and stalagmites everywhere. Now standing upright she stretched out her aching arms and back and took in the majestic cave. She had never been one for tight spaces but being inside the very cave system that was home to an extinct hominin species, was simply exhilarating. Sam's face played across her mind. He would have appreciated this. A lump formed in her throat and she wiped her face with the inside of her shirt and cleared her throat.

"Ok Alex, let's get that tooth and get the hell out of here," she spoke words of encouragement to herself. The beam of her flashlight looked into every angle for clues as she searched the cave. If the professor had hidden the tooth here it could be anywhere, but what she knew for certain was that she had followed his clues — she just needed to find the next one.

"Think Alex, think. Where would he hide the tooth?"

Up to now the professor had used authentic ancient riddles. He was a paleoanthropologist so chances were he'd communicate through fossils. She searched the floor bed, pacing every inch of the cave. Eventually her torch settled on a corner where a small pile of fossil bones lay to one side as if it was the remains after a lion's hunt. Alex bent down to inspect it. Her memory flashed to the fake bone Ezra found in the professor's office and she picked them up, one by one. All in all there were about twenty bones — vertebrae, possible parts of a ribcage, a few digits, and then a large femur. Working her way through each bone checking for anything peculiar she paused when a noise came from inside one of the digit bones. She shook it vigorously from side to side. There was something inside. She spat on the bone and rubbed it clean with her shirt to reveal a bone mimicking the very rubber-ized PVC bone they had found the first clue in. Ecstatic with the find Alex twisted the ends in opposite directions and heard the familiar click and release. Barely able to contain her excite-ment she carefully pulled the two ends apart and tipped them over into the palm of her shaking hand. Her heart drummed against her chest as two molars stared back at her.

CHAPTER TWENTY-TWO

The difficult crawl back to the cave entrance was propelled by overwhelming euphoria. Alex couldn't stop smiling. With intoxicating pride and newfound energy, she navigated her way back through the tight underground cave system. She'd give Volkov the tooth so he'd let Sam go, and once she was back home, ICCRU would hunt him down. He wasn't her problem anymore. She had found what she was sent there for. All she cared about now was Sam — and getting out of there alive.

When she finally stepped foot into the hole again, she tugged on the rope, signaling for Volkov's men to pull her up.

"Pull me up, Volkov! I have what you want!" She yelled up into the opening above her head. The sun had already set and the moon's dim light shone down on her.

"Hey, Volkov! Get your goons to lift me out!" She shouted again when nothing happened, tugging on the rope at the same time.

"It's over Volkov! Drop the gun."

Alex recognized Matthew Fletcher's voice echoing down the hole. Relieved her heart beat rapidly against her chest and she lowered her head into her hands. It's all over. ICCRU had found her and had come to her rescue.

"Matt! I'm down here!" She shouted upwards again.

Loose dirt dropped onto her face as she stared at the open hole above her head. A man's silhouette blocked the moonlight and Alex felt the rope around her waist tighten.

Heat radiated from her heart and Alex eagerly grabbed hold of the rope above her head. As the moon's light grew closer and closer Alex suppressed a smile. Her insides leaped with joy as her head ascended over the lip of the hole. Barely on her feet and still in a crawling position, Volkov's six foot five accomplice, jerked her body upright, and before Alex knew it, Volkov's arm had her in a vice-like grip with his gun to her head while his accomplice sliced the rope off her body.

"I said, drop your gun Volkov. It's the end of the road for you. Let her go." Matt's stern voice commanded Volkov.

Volkov looked around as he moved back toward his men.

"Never, Matthew Fletcher, never!"

Without warning Matt's gun fired three shots; its sound piercing the night sky. Alex flinched assuming he was shooting at Volkov only to find his three accomplices fall to their knees instead.

"You're next, Volkov! Let her go!" Matt repeated.

Volkov's arm tightened around Alex's neck as he dragged her away from Matt.

"We could do this together, you know Matt. Like the good old days. What happened in Berlin wasn't my doing, and you know it."

"Berlin? What does he mean, Matt?" Alex asked confused.

"Yes Matt. What do I mean? Tell her. Tell her how long we go back and that you're not the goody two shoes you're professing to be."

"This is your last chance, Volkov. Let her go or my next bullet is in your brain."

"You won't shoot your best friend, Matt. I've known you long enough to know you don't have the guts. Let us go. No one will ever know and your cherished reputation will remain unscathed. Besides, you shoot me and my gun will fire off a bullet through our precious little gem's brain before the bullet hits me."

"That's ok by me. I have no use for her anymore; only the tooth."

Alex drew back a sharp breath as her jaw dropped open.

"What the hell are you doing, Matt?"

"Well, well, what do you know? A leopard doesn't change its spots. So you're just like me after all, aren't you Matty-boy?"

"Matt! What the hell is he talking about? Do something!"

"ICCRU's turned dirty, Alex. Newsflash, Matt's not here to save you. He's after the tooth too."

"What? No. Matt's here to save me from you. He sent me on this mission."

"Oh you naïve little thing. He's crooked, Alex. He couldn't figure out where the tooth was hidden on his own so he got you to do it for him. He used you, Alex and he used ICCRU as a smokescreen.

"But you kidnapped Sam."

"I didn't kidnap your darling boyfriend, Alex. That guy in the video footage was one of my men who betrayed me. I needed you to get into that hole, and that was all I could think about at the time."

"Sam's alive and safe?"

"I guess so."

"Yeah well, not quite actually. I couldn't have him expose me," Matt spoke.

Matt's words crushed her insides.

"So it's true? Volkov is right. You're a crook."

"Crook is a bit of a harsh word, but hey, what do I care? Did you honestly think I would let an opportunity as big as this pass me by? Do you know how long I've waited for something like this to happen? Year after year I recover ancient paintings and valuable artifacts only for them to be locked away in a vault or a museum somewhere. It's worth more money than what I can make in three lifetimes behind my desk."

"So you're doing this for money?" Alex asked, angry.

"What else is there? I'll be sipping Piña coladas on a white sandy beach somewhere far from here for the rest of my life."

"Where's Sam?" Alex whispered as tears stung her eyes.

"If it's money you're after Fletcher, I'll double what you think you can get for it," Volkov interrupted before Matt could answer.

"I already have my buyer, Volkov. Besides this provides me with the perfect opportunity to get rid of you for good."

Volkov pulled his grip tighter around Alex's neck as he moved backward. His foot stumbled on the body of one of his men and he lost his balance; letting go of Alex as he fell back. His gun fired a shot in the air above his head and Alex ducked, escaping behind the tree. Her hand reached for her gun in the nape of her back only to remember that Volkov had removed both her and Ezra's guns before sending her down the hole.

Matt fired a shot at Volkov, killing him instantly and then turned to pursue Alex.

"Give me the tooth, Alex. There's no way you can escape me. How do you think I found you in the first place?"

Stunned Alex ran and hid behind the next tree, using the dark shadows to her advantage. She pondered on his words. He did find her, yes. How? Her mind raced but it finally came to her. He must have planted a tracking device. Shielded by the tree she patted down her body and legs and stopped at her belt. She yanked it from her pants and found the tiny tracker hidden in the buckle. *Bastard*, she thought. She tied it around the tree trunk and darted to the next one.

"There's no way in hell I'm letting you get away, Alex. I have too much riding on this deal."

From behind the tree Alex stared out into the dark night. She couldn't see Matt anymore and he had gone silent. She pushed her back and head against the tree and shut her eyes as she took a deep breath. Still he said nothing. She popped her head around the tree on either side but he was nowhere to be found. Deciding to make a run for it she tightened her leg muscles and set her sights on another tree ten yards away. She bolted and almost instantly a bullet sliced through the air over her head. She kept running, jumping over several rocks in her way. Another bullet whisked past her ear causing her to divert in the opposite direction. Behind her she heard Matt's feet thump down hard as he chased her across the open grassland. There were no more trees to hide behind so she zigzagged across the field in an attempt to throw him off his aim.

But it did her no good and he came at her fast and furious. Her foot stepped into a pothole and she heard the chilling sound of her ankle breaking as she fell hard to the ground. Pain radiated up her leg as she scrambled to her feet in an effort to keep running, but it was impossible. She was unable to stand on her foot. Desperate she looked around for him and used her arms and one leg to crawl across the field. Panic flooded her veins as she clambered in a futile attempt to get away from him. And before she could crawl another inch, Matt's large hand pushed down hard on her back and her cheek slammed into the dirt.

"Where's the tooth, Alex? I know you have it."

Alex squirmed with pain as he pushed her face harder onto the ground.

"I don't have it. It's in the cave."

"Give it to me or I'll kill you right now, Alex!"

"You're going to kill me anyway."

Matt let go of her head and flipped her onto her back. With his gun pointed at her face he threatened her again.

"I'll blow a hole in each of your legs and then your body until you tell me where that tooth is, Alex. Starting with this leg first."

Terrified, Alex watched Matt take aim at her unimpaired leg. The cracking sound of a bullet filled the air and Alex let out a frantic scream before Matt fell face first on top of her. His large body knocked her wind out and pinned her head between his shoulder and the ground. Unable to see she pushed to get him off. Frantic thoughts engulfed her when she realized Volkov might have survived the earlier shooting and she wrestled to free herself.

As if in a dream, Sam's face appeared as he pulled Matt's body off hers. A wave of surprised but equal relief washed over her as Sam buried her head in his shoulder.

"How did you find me?" She sobbed.

"Shh, it's all over now, my love. You know I'm never far behind."

An hour later Alex lay on a gurney as they loaded her into the ambulance.

"Congratulations, Miss Hunt." Jean-Pierre DuPont leaned in

moments before the medics lifted her into the ambulance. "What you've accomplished here today is of immense proportions. We always suspected Ivan Volkov was too good to be true, but exposing Matt Fletcher as a traitor while retrieving the missing piece of history? Well, that's nothing short of exceptional."

"Monsieur DuPont, back there Volkov mentioned he and Matt had a history together, something about Berlin. What was he talking about?"

"As it turns out, they started off together in the CIA. Matt and Volkov were best friends. But on a mission in Berlin something went wrong and Matt's wife was killed in an explosion which Matt believed Volkov was behind. He left the CIA and started working for ICCRU. Needless to say their friendship ceased and since then, Matt's been hell-bent on a vendetta to expose Volkov."

"Seems he had his own agenda with the tooth though," Sam commented. "He gave me quite a whack on the head back at the farm."

"How did you find me, Sam? How did you know where I was?"

"It seems our friend Fletcher planted a tracking device on you. He had it all planned out; made it look like he was one of the good guys. I guess he didn't bargain on Volkov derailing his plans."

Alex smiled as Sam planted a kiss on her head.

"Oh, Monsieur DuPont, I think you're forgetting something."

She reached into her pocket and pulled out the rubberized PVC bone and shook it.

"What's this?" DuPont stared at the fake bone looking puzzled.

"Open it."

DuPont fiddled with it and finally twisted it open. The teeth rolled out onto his palm.

"TWO! You got us two molars? We were hoping for one, but two! That's phenomenal."

A nd when DuPont finally left their side and excitedly secured the teeth in UNESCO's mobile unit, Sam leaned over and whispered in Alex's ear.

"Think the time has come for you to say yes."

T he ALEX HUNT Adventures continue in The DAUPHIN DECEPTION. Available in eBook and Paperback **(https://books2read.com/THE-DAUPHIN-DECEPTION)**

A boy-king the world never knew about. A missing relic said to have proven his death. An unknown enemy with a deadly secret.

When a series of anonymous letters lure archaeologists Alex and Sam into a hidden world of secrets, they are thrust into a dangerous game of cat-and-mouse. In too deep and fighting for survival, they soon realize there's no turning back. Plunged into a world where no one can be trusted, the illustrious team face the powers and wrath of a dangerous secret fraternity that has ruled the world for centuries.

Dating back to the French Revolution with its members said to include the most influential leaders in the world, the order will stop at nothing to bury its secrets deep within the vaults of history. Now, it is up to Alex and Sam to beat them at their own game and expose the truth.

Will the clandestine brotherhood manage to exert their power and continue to deceive the world, or have they met their match?

Another action-packed Adventure Thriller that will have you at the edge of your seat! This is the fourth page-turning book in the Alex Hunt Adventure Thriller series.

Inspired by true historical facts and events. Also suitable as a standalone novel.

*Includes Bonus content and a free digital copy of the series prequel.

Receive a FREE copy of the prequel and see where it all started!

NOT AVAILABLE ANYWHERE ELSE!

Click on image or enter http://download.urcelia.com in your browser

MORE BOOKS BY URCELIA TEIXEIRA

ALEX HUNT Adventure Thrillers

Also suited as standalone novels

The PAPUA INCIDENT - Prequel (sign up to get it FREE)

The RHAPTA KEY

The GILDED TREASON

The ALPHA STRAIN

The DAUPHIN DECEPTION

The BARI BONES

The CAIAPHAS CODE

FREE BONUS - BEHIND THE BOOK

Download this FREE FACT FILE on Homo naledi and the research behind this book!

View actual photos from the discovery and excavation and go underground through a virtual video tour in the Sterkfontein Caves.

Value added information on South African politics,

Apartheid as well as the author's depiction of the characters from this book!

Click image and download (or type in http://bit.ly/Get-Factfile)

Thank you for purchasing my book. If you enjoyed this book, I would sincerely appreciate it if you could take the time to **leave a review**. It would mean so much to me!

For sneak previews, free books and more,
Join my mailing list

No-Spam Newsletter
ELITE SQUAD

FOLLOW Urcelia Teixeira

BookBub has a New Release Alert. Not only can you check out the latest deals, but you can also get an email when I release my next book by following me here

https://www.bookbub.com/authors/urcelia-teixeira

Website:
https://www.urcelia.com

Facebook:
https://www.facebook.com/urceliabooks

Twitter:
https//www.twitter.com/UrceliaTeixeira

BEHIND THE BOOK - AUTHOR NOTES

Based on the true discovery

On Friday September 13, 2013 two recreational cavers, Rick Hunter and Steven Tucker accidentally discovered a bed of mysterious fossil bones thirty meters underground in an unchartered cave just outside Johannesburg, South Africa.

Professor Lee Berger, a paleoanthropologist and National Geographic Explorer led the excavation of over 1550 fossil bones belonging to a unique hominin species later dubbed Homo *naledi*.

Six female archaeologists arrived at the Rising Star cave some two months later. Braving the arduous and treacherous unexplored cave system, they set about unearthing the bones millimeter by millimeter, even using toothpicks and porcupine quills as part of their equipment.

On September 10, 2015, the University of Witwatersrand, South Africa formally unveiled, for the first time ever, a unique new human relative to our family tree. The significance of Homo *naledi's* discovery turned science on its head when it provided DNA evidence of its close relation to humans as we are today, claiming its existence as young as between 200,000 and 300,000 years ago.

To see photos of the actual excavation, and the author's research

Download your Homo naledi fact file here now

ABOUT THE AUTHOR

Urcelia Teixeira is an author of fast-paced archaeological action-adventure novels with a Christian nuance.

Her Alex Hunt Adventure Thriller Series has been described by readers as 'Indiana Jones meets Lara Croft with a twist of Bourne'. She read her first book when she was four and wrote her first poem when she was seven. And though she lived vicariously through books, and her far too few travels, life happened. She married the man of her dreams and birthed three boys (and added two dogs, a cat, three chickens, and some goldfish!) So, life became all about settling down and providing a means to an end. She climbed the corporate ladder, exercised her entrepreneurial flair and made her mark in real estate.

Traveling and exploring the world made space for child-friendly annual family holidays by the sea. The ones where she succumbed to building sandcastles and barely got past reading the first five pages of a book. And on the odd occasion she managed to read fast enough to page eight, she was confronted with a moral dilemma as the umpteenth expletive forced its way off just about every page!

But by divine intervention, upon her return from yet another male-dominated camping trip, when fifty knocked hard and fast on her door, and she could no longer stomach the profanities in her reading material, she drew a line in the sand and bravely set off to create a new adventure!

It was in the dark, quiet whispers of the night, well past midnight late in the year 2017, that Alex Hunt was born.

Her philosophy

From her pen flow action-packed adventures for the armchair traveler who enjoys a thrilling escape. Devoid of the usual profanity and obscenities, she incorporates real-life historical relics and mysteries from exciting places all over the world. She aims to kidnap her reader from the mundane and plunge them into feel-good riddle-solving quests filled with danger, sabotage, and mystery!

For more visit www.urcelia.com or email her on books@urcelia.com

facebook.com/urceliateixeira

twitter.com/urcelia_teixeira

instagram.com/urceliateixeira

COPYRIGHT © 2019 BY URCELIA TEIXEIRA

Paperback © ISBN: 978-0-6399665-7-1

Independently Published by Urcelia Teixeira

www.urcelia.com

books@urcelia.com

Made in the USA
Monee, IL
31 July 2020